Dream

Bells

Violeta Mateeva

Certain real agencies, pesticide-related terms, conventions and places are mentioned in this novel. However, the story and the characters in it are entirely fictitious.

ISBN 979-8-8496-9011-7

Chapter 1
Erie

I could see nearly all of it out of my bedroom window, perched at the very top of the swan house. Has it ever felt like *home*, I wondered, *ever*?

For as long as I could remember, my favourite Stellaria had been that other town-the town in my mother's bedtime stories, sparkling in fireworks of creativity. There had been a baker then who'd invented the cheese-apricot waffle, a rainbow-chocolate maker, a tailor crafting singing neckties, and of course, my granddad. He'd been the architect behind that utter defiance of straight lines and right angles that our town had become.

An illusion-like, breathtakingly beautiful.

The first house he'd built, etching the memory of his strong hands into the white convex walls, was now my family's home. Smooth and effortless, it flowed from the ground towards the skies. The closed-winged body below swelled over the first two levels then narrowed, morphing into ornamental, neckline structure. Dotted with glassed openings, the structure joined at its other end to the uppermost room. That room reclined over the rest of the house like a swan's head.

Despite the whiteness outside, or maybe because of it, the inside was full of colours. The entrance opened into a small toffee hallway. An archway on the right led to the green-and-cream sitting room, another one, on the left–to the aqua kitchen. A wooden spiral staircase rose to the left of the entrance to take you to the bedrooms above. One was red-gold and the other–lilac-silver. Then finally, a smaller staircase swirled into the topmost room with its swan eyes: the outwards flexing windows.

The spruce tree on the other side of the glass swayed its green splays as if trying to come in, to warm up by the wood stove. Normally we didn't stoke up the stove that early in the autumn but the weather had turned biting. If it kept going this way, the slanting black tiles on the roof above me were in for a barrage of snow before long.

Pat. Pat. Pat. I could hear Mum's gentle steps pattering on the staircase, coming up closer and closer. In a moment she would peep through the door and check on me, hoping that the essay I'd been working on for the past hour had miraculously finished itself. Her voice would sound cheerful; her soul would be, as always, hopeful.

'All done, Erie?' mum asked. 'I could help you with the presentation, you know, before dinner.'

I had one last peek through the window and turned around. 'Thanks mum, but I've still got some writing to do. The opponents' case.'

'Socrates?'

'Plato actually, his student, and Aristotle.' I decided to talk for a while to mum, to reassure her of my enthusiasm. After all, rhetoric was Stellaria's pride and joy, the main curriculum subject which was inexcusable not to have a liking for.

'They are the best known philosophers of Ancient Greece: Plato, Socrates and Aristotle. Brilliant rhetoricians too,' I explained for mum's benefit. She'd been fortunate enough to study completely ordinary subjects in secondary school: maths, for example, and geography and history. No rhetoric, that is, the art of eloquent speaking (also called oration) and writing.

'They advocated good rhetoric which is logical and based only on facts. Also, it isn't done for money or fame, by twisting the truth. I admire them for that.'

Mum nodded in agreement. She placed a soothing hand over my shoulder as I sat down at my study desk. 'We could all learn from the masters, dear. He's your favourite though, Socrates, isn't he?'

'Yes…' I nodded slightly. Bitter and sharp, I felt the resentment rising inside my throat. 'Do you know, people often remember him only by how he died? He was sentenced by a court to take a hemlock poison. But I think that his life was more important. '*No one does wrong willingly, but only out of ignorance*': that's what he believed.'

Mum's face tensed. Her eyebrows scrunched up in a wary, grave thought while she remained silent for a few moments. 'That's a *dangerous* idea,' she finally said.

No, I shook my head. *No*. There were dangers to it, of course, ways to abuse it, to excuse criminal behaviour. But there was also deep humanity running underneath the idea that knowledge could right all the wrongs in the world. It took courage to believe in people *that* much.

'Maybe,' I replied. My gaze met Mum's: an identical blend of a hazel's leafy green and mellow brown. 'But it comes from a compassionate heart…'

Mum soon returned downstairs to put the finishing touches to the beef casserole simmering on the hob for dinner. I thought how good it could have been to lend her a hand. To inhale the magic of the fragrant kitchen spices...To dissolve all my heart's hurt, all its crushing desperation, into the wispy weightlessness of the aromas: tarragon, cloves and peppercorns ...

Write! Write, if you can, whinging fool! The essay paper stared me straight in the eye. Implacable, chillingly white, it dared me to fill it page after page, with oration brilliance.

There had been many days like this one, many similar assignments. Stellaria's educational system was gruelling. It produced accomplished orators by the end of secondary school, demanding a written essay every weekday and oral presentation on a teacher's request as often as four times a week. My peers were the shining proof of success. They didn't need to practise at home anymore; they could give a dazzling speech just like that, at the drop of a hat. Why couldn't I? Well, in my case that hat was rather cumbersome and took ages to drop from the heights of my black-haired head. It encountered too many thoughts, too many connections on the way.

Lately, I caught myself scanning through the eager faces of my classmates in lessons, wondering about something. How did we become so oration-mad? Our entire town? Kids debated on the streets instead of skipping rope or playing hide-and-seek.

Toddlers were scolded for doing 'fatuous' things just because the word sounded much more fanciful than 'silly'. Even Senstar, the chocolate factory, had an oration training programme and breaks for 'improvement of staff communication'.

I remember dad saying once that we, Stellarians, had always had an intense sense of solidarity. A love for doing things as a town…

Could I blame this love for all my days and years filled with anguish?

Chapter 2
Senstar

Angelina Bell had been working in the chocolate factory for 20 happy years, with an ever increasing sense of pride and accomplishment. She had witnessed, ever since her childhood, Stellaria's transformation into the 'heritage site of breath-taking beauty, swan-like houses in the shadow of Ben Nevis and hand-crafted, rainbow chocolates,' that travel brochures advertised. Unlike the cities competing in donning uniform mantles of glass-cold skyscrapers and Wi-Fi, Stellaria had always had her own character. At the heart of its prosperity and uniqueness was Senstar.

The chilly, mid-September day began with urgent letters, delivered to all employees by a messenger boy. A little after eight o'clock Angelina Bell reached an office at the back of Senstar. The sign on it read 'Philius Sento, Director'. The secretary's 'Good morning, Mrs Bell' was professionally lukewarm and Angelina was motioned to proceed beyond a second door.

The director was dressed in an expensively tailored grey suit. He was sitting behind a mahogany desk where a pile of papers lay over green velvet. An ornate, mother-of-pearl stationary box was open to reveal a collection of fountain pens. The grandeur of the huge landscape paintings hanging on the walls and the office's leather furnishing were well chosen to deliver the message of their owner: Philius Sento was a force not to be trifled with.

'It is very good to see you, Mrs Bell, very good. Please, sit down.'

The director indicated the luxurious armchair opposite him. The glib smile he wore didn't reach his dark, hawk-like eyes. 'As you have already been informed, an emergency committee has been set up to oversee the debates in the matter of the city scientist. When I thought of an esteemed, reliable and highly capable person to chair that committee, I knew there could not possibly be anybody else suited better for the position than you, my dear Mrs Bell. I have complete confidence in your serving Senstar's interests with distinguished expertise.'

Angelina gave a short, business-like nod, sitting even straighter in the brown leather armchair. A bond began forging between her and the director now, the sort of bond allies feel before launching into a fight.

'You will recall that the scientist,' Sento continued, 'received our full cooperation when he first arrived. He requested to examine the entire documentation on the cocoa purchase. I obliged. Then he took samples of our cocoa to send for chemical analyses in London. I allowed it in good faith. Senstar and I as its director have demonstrated nothing but professionalism on our part as chocolatiers par excellence. The scientist however, I must regretfully say, has failed to respond with due regard for our world-renowned enterprise. He has disrupted the smooth operation of the factory!'

The director suddenly lurched forward, arching his fingers like claws over the desk's mahogany. His eyes blazed with malice. The smoothness of him was now all gone, all drained out within a couple of heartbeats.

'This morning he had the audacity to come here, to my office, and claim that our cocoa is-', Sento spat out the word like the foulest thing imaginable, *'poisonous*! He practically *demanded* that we STOP the production!'

The force of his words was such that it took Angelina aback, physically pushing her further into the armchair. The leather around her became quicksand. She felt like falling, falling down a bottomless chasm. Her arms went limp; when she spoke, the words came out slowly, in laboured gasps.

'I... just... can't believe it. Senstar... has never been closed...never in fifty years!'

Opposite her, Sento was already morphing back into composure. Regretting his outburst, the director leaned back in the lush armchair and hid the black-tar anger behind the mask of calm authority. Once again he was in control. He was the man who could foresee every obstacle on the road ahead and deal with it. The conclusion of his meeting then followed, done in a true Stellarian style:

'Phantasmal his assertions are, Mrs Bell, truly incomprehensible to the rational mind. It is our duty and yours, as a chairwoman, to refute his allegations and defend the honourable name of our town. Poison in our cocoa?! A pesticide toxic to fish, and our kidneys and livers?! It couldn't be anything but a conjecture in such a pristine and beautiful place as Stellaria.'

Angelina defended Senstar's reputation as she chaired an hour of orating both before noon and in the early evening. With the entire staff assembled in the packing room, Philius Sento was the first to deliver his speech on the factory's safety procedures and outstanding safety record. The manager, Rob Thomson's talk followed, on the issue of Stellaria's right of self-governance. His ending words of 'We will not tolerate city know-it-alls telling us what to do or not to do in our own town' were met with enthusiastic applause.

The last person to take to the podium (speeches scheduled under the director's instructions), was the scientist.

'Thank you for giving me the opportunity to explain my findings,' the scientist began. He looked at the unfriendly, scowling faces in front of him and felt ill at ease. The Stellarians seemed to be glaring beyond his young, bookish looks, beyond his measured words into some unseen threat. 'As you know, the cocoa from the factory has been analysed in our lab in London. What we have been measuring is pesticide residues. They are small but potentially dangerous amounts of pesticides that remain in the cocoa beans after harvest. 'How do the pesticides get there in the first place?' you might ask. Well, the cocoa trees are sprayed against pests. Then some pesticides fall directly on the cocoa pods while others are absorbed through the tree roots and leaves. Using high-precision gas chromatographs we determine–'

An irate voice sounded amongst the workers:

'What does all this science mumbo-jumbo have to do with us?'

‘We’ve been making chocolates for fifty years, mister; nobody has complained of any bloody poison before,’ shouted an old, wizened lady, who had been packing rainbow shapes for longer than she could remember.

‘That is because the cocoa you used before was from a good, uncontaminated batch. The new one isn’t! I’ve been doing-‘

‘Slandering our factory, that’s what you’ve been doing! Smearing our town! Spinning far-fetched tales!’

The hall erupted in a cacophony of yells-accusing, taunting, threatening. The resentment rose like a tidal wave and pressed on the scientist, making him sway backwards, almost losing his balance. He lifted his arms, palms opened against the multitude of workers and pleaded for understanding.

‘Please, let me explain…‘

Sitting behind a table on his left, Angelina brought down the gavel in her hand-one, two, three times. In the restored silence she turned towards the scientist, her expression severe. ‘Be brief, sir, ’she said.

His voice strained now, the scientists made an effort to continue. He wished the workers could understand. He wished they knew he was on their side. The danger was hanging over their heads, for goodness sake. There was endosulfan in their cocoa, he explained, an extremely toxic pesticide that was banned in the 127 countries of the Stockholm Convention on Persistent Organic Pollutants (POPs). And that wasn't all. The residual endosulfan in the chocolate that Stellarians produced and consumed every day, was in fact in alarmingly high concentration. Three times higher than what was considered a safe daily intake.'

'This is an outrage,' thundered the voice of Rob Thomson, the manager. 'Never has our factory been so insulted!'

'The nerve of him! How dare he!' Outcries of protest erupted around the hall. They crackled, picked up power like tongues of fire leaping out from a heap of hazardously dry logs.

From his place at the back of the room Philius Sento observed the scientist's escape with a canny, satisfied smile. He had judged him to be good at his job of collecting samples and analysing but pitifully inept at the art of oration. A cripple, as far as social skills were concerned. Today they'd seen the proof of that. When accommodatingly 'given the opportunity' to speak in front of the factory's workforce, the fellow had spectacularly failed.

Philius Sento, on the other hand, had weighed up his options carefully. Not long ago he had purchased a vast supply of cocoa at a very lucrative price, in fact, two times below the market value. He had no intention of replacing it with a new one. But if Sento had ignored the scientist's warnings and said nothing about it to the staff, the scientist would have returned to his city desk and kept sending pestilential reports to the mayor, to the government, to who knows who else. He, Sento, and he alone, would have been blamed in these reports for not dealing with the environmental threat.

Well, now this wasn't going to happen. Philius Sento had judged well. Whoever came next to throw wild accusations around here would have the entire factory to contend with. And soon the entire town.

Chapter 3
Fears

A short, nervous knock sounded on my bedroom door. I stopped trying to extricate my navy school jumper from under the arts & crafts chest; then turned around to see mum's sombre face at the door.

'Erie, I have to leave early today. Will you be alright getting breakfast on your own? '

'Of course, mum. Making toast with jam is hardly rocket science. ' I took a few steps towards her, noticed the streaks of anxiety in her eyes. 'What's happening at the factory? Mum? How serious is it?'

'We have...a situation. But not to worry, there isn't anything dangerous,' she said. 'You get yourself ready now; I'll know more when I come back.'

Her words left me unsettled. To me, words had always been much more than mere clusters of sounds. They were waves of emotions undulating in subtle hues, or exploding with force, or streaming in intermingling colours of happiness, sadness, angst and fear. Healing words, or hurting; words infused with a myriad of meanings over the span between the white of the logical sense and the black of its opposite… I knew, instantly, that mum's 'not to worry' meant a serious cause for concern. The tension in her tone was a sign of imminent battle. Against whom?

Relentlessly, the images and questions duelled in my mind. Breakfast, collecting my school stuff, wrapping in the waterproof, blue jacket and making the short walk to the school on the fifth Necklace Hill-the factory's chimney belching a foul-smelling, poisonous smoke, forests in yellowing agony, workers unconscious on the packing room floor, city hospitals stretched to the limit. No, it couldn't be happening; I was surely overreacting…

That day the fears about the factory somehow shielded me from all the heartache that school was, had always been for me. Ever since my first day in Mrs Zinnia's class. In these classrooms sheltered from the elements by black roof tiles, along these white, colonnaded corridors forming a rectangle around a fountain courtyard, daggers of stares and words had been bleeding, drop after drop, my self-confidence for many long years.

'Hey there, oration genius,' called out to me a tall, pale-gold-haired girl. Jay Libertia, her green eyes alive with jibing sparks. 'Are we going to be treated to one of your masterpieces today? On rhetoric in Ancient Greece? I can't wait.'

My best line of defence, as I knew quite well from eternity of practice, was to ignore it all. There couldn't possibly be a way for me to enter an oration fight and win it. But today…today I could afford to throw at least a punch.

'Has it occurred to you that rhetoric isn't everything, Jay? '

I stepped into the classroom, Jay walking beside me and keeping up quite well with my fast pace. I threw a chilling look in her direction before taking my seat at the back. 'That there are real dangers out there to be *dealt with*, not simply talked about?'

Jay's answer came as troubled silence.

Nightmare poison scenarios were almost rolling like a horror movie in my head by the time I escaped the madness of the lunchtime oration. I set off for the northern side of the building. Leaving the school premises wasn't allowed, of course, but I'd found a way to slip out unnoticed. There was a gap in the hedge border that stood between the school and the forest extending up the hillside. My secret place was just ten steps away under an old spruce tree, whose branches formed a sort of a green tent round its rugged trunk.

Finally I could have my cheese-and- lettuce sandwich in complete silence and blissful peace…

'So, that's where you disappear during lunch break! Cosy spot, though a little bit prickly,' Jay said, drawing aside the splays of green needles like curtains and taking a seat on the ground next to me. She peered into my face with curiosity:

'What's up with you, Erie? Your oration today wasn't nearly as amusingly bad as it used to be.'

'Jay, I swear, if you are here to lecture me again…'

'No, no, just the usual, elevated Stellarian conversation…But listen, there's something I want to ask you about. Fay, my sister, works at Senstar, in the mixing room, the same as your mum. But you know that, don't you? '

Half annoyed at Jay's sneaking in, half relieved to have somebody to talk to, I threw an uncertain glance in her direction. I gave her a short nod for an answer. Over the last couple of years Jay had been a peculiar kind of a friendly foe to me. Somebody I could actually have a conversation with. She urged me, of course, to show a little bit more than a morsel of enthusiasm for oration but she also listened to my stories about the things I enjoyed. Jay was always candid: in both of her disapproval and her amused interest. I somehow liked her for that. The rest of my class could only relish poisonous comments behind my back.

'Fay left early for work this morning in a hurry. I can tell she was worried. What's your mum saying?' Jay asked.

'That there's nothing dangerous. But that's just what adults say, thinking we can't take the truth.'

'Did she mention the poisoning?'

Jay looked at me, noticing the shake of my head: No. She shuffled, feeling no doubt the chill of the autumn ground beneath her, then folded arms over her bent knees.

'There must be something more to it. The way I see it, if our chocolates are poisonous, this will spell trouble for an awful lot of people. One,' she counted on the fingers of her hand, 'nearly the entire town works at Senstar. If something happens to it, most people will be out of a job. Including Mr Sento. Two, the entire town gorges on chocolates, so we could all be poisoned, and three, we export to the City- to all these rich and famous with sweet tooth. I think-'

'You think,' I gasped in realisation,' Mr Sento is lying about it!

Jay rolled her eyes at me. '*He is likely to downplay the danger involved*, that's what a true rhetorician would say, Erie.' She sighed. 'But yes, he might and he probably will… 'What we are going to witness from now on will probably be a total smoke screen.'

Later, safely snuggled on the sofa at home, I needed to wait just a couple of hours more before my questions began to be answered. A little after five o'clock in the evening Mum burst through the door of our swan cottage.

'What a day! ' she exclaimed. 'What a day!'

Mum zoomed in the living room on the last dregs of agitated energy and dropped exhausted into a seat next to Dad. The cream-leather sofa they were now both sitting on was opposite me, across the green-patterned cream rug covering the wooden floor. Shadows of flames flickered and danced over it. The fireplace on my left crackled, seeping its warmth into the room.

'Angel!' Dad smiled tenderly. 'An eventful day, wasn't it? Senstar is in a bit of a tight spot, I hear.'

'Yes… and no. Nothing that we can't handle, Nicolas.'

Then she started proudly listing all the speeches made at the factory: Mr Sento, Mr Thomson…la-di-da-fifteen in all! And neither of them had been even remotely related to the most important thing!

'Mum, but what about the POISONING? ' I finally cried out.

'Oh, that turned out to be the rather implausible and vague story of that impetuous fellow, the scientist,' Mum replied. Her usually soft, gentle face now had a hardened look. It made me think of a mother cat ready to spring onto every dark shadow threatening her litter of meowing kittens.

'He's insisting that the factory closes down until the cocoa is replaced with a new batch. Imagine! The entire factory shut down only because some officials, sitting at their desks somewhere, came up with some rules that even they are not sure about.'

'Not sure? What do you mean, Angel?' Dad asked bemused.

'Apparently, our cocoa has these pesticide residues and they are three times more than what some regulations say. But what would happen when they are three times higher? Nothing, that's what. We are talking about some really small, minute, infinitesimal amounts that might or might not cause illnesses fifty years from now.'

'It can't be that simple, mum. Scientists must have done enough tests on animals,' I joined in, 'so, they can find out the safe limits.'

'Oh, yes,' she waved the idea aside, dismissively. 'We all know how these science fellows are-they do their experiments, come up with theories. Their theories change ever so often-according to the agenda of the day. One day they say that something is dangerous, the next day that it's completely innocuous... Do you know, one of my co-workers even expressed concerns that the allegations of poisoning could be an attempt to sabotage the planned exports to the sea coast? There is a rival chocolate factory there.'

'Ah, that must be it! You at the factory turn everything into an offensive against Stellaria. ' Dad's expression turned sombre. Something about being a doctor, now the town's senior one, had made him very careful about forming quick opinions. Many diseases had similar symptoms; they could be easily confused with each other. And so were people's intentions. Very often you couldn't fathom them unless you looked at the wider picture.

'Angel,' he reasoned, 'the guy could be just doing his job- he could be concerned about health risks. I can understand this as a doctor who sees illness every day. '

'The management doesn't think so and neither do I.' Mum's eyes flashed with familiar, 'chocolate factory' zeal and her voice turned a pitch higher. 'We've been making the best chocolate in the country without a hint of trouble for fifty years! We intend to keep it that way!'

Well, there is nothing for it, but patience and time, Dad's knowing eyes told me. We both were very well aware of mum's fierce pride in Senstar. It had been not only her workplace for the last twenty years but her second home as well.

Dad's face lit in one of his brilliant smiles that melted worries away as fast as a booming stove thawed ice cubes.

'Why don't we postpone all the serious talk for after dinner?' he said brightly, 'We are all starving, aren't we? And I've brought some scrumptious strawberry tarts from Mrs Phlox.'

Whiffs of homemade stew were soon drifting in the living room to announce one of my favourite times of the day. Unlike my peers who were made to ponder on polemical techniques and chew their food in silence, dinner was always cheerful at our house. I could speak to my parents about things that worried me; about books I loved reading (not the ones on oration!). I could also listen to stories or laugh at jokes told around the walnut dining table. This evening it was the story of the carpenter, Mr Penstemon's cat. The cat had turned out to be a budding artist: he had carved modernistic designs of scratches on the wooden chairs meant for the Town Hall offices. So, Mr Penstemon had stormed into the GP surgery that day, fuming. His pet had some kind of disorder, yes, yes, hyperactivity, most definitely! Were there any cat medicines for that? Ehm, no, my dad had said. But locking the workshop from now on should nip all these artistic impulses in the bud.

As the night strewed the sky with glittering stars, I climbed the stairs to my room, relieved. My heart could only feel content here, behind the dark wooden door; between the windows with magnificently *distant* views of Stellaria. Mobiles of origami birds hung from the ceiling, gently swaying in the air rippled by my steps. Paintings of fairies came alive in the moonlight piercing the window glass. Silvery shapes that I'd printed over the blue voile canopy of my four-poster bed echoed the wonder of the night sky.

This was a room like no other. A room where *oration was exiled* to a single, unremarkable, unloved, plain bookshelf over the study desk.

Chapter 4
Fire of oration

Within a day Stellaria was on fire: incensed, riled, belligerent, engulfed in the most ferocious of debates. The town square turned into the focus of it all, a polemic stage from which a hot deluge of speeches poured day and night. Patriotic pride in Stellaria's achievements was daily chanted here, human over aquatic creatures' rights were proclaimed, chemical analyses were decried and a shadow of suspicion over the scientist's credentials was darkly cast.

There was no way he had arrived in Stellaria with good intentions. He was an outsider, an ignoramus, ruining the factory's excellent reputation to his own selfish ends.

'If only he wasn't such an unpleasant fellow…' carried voices over the cobbled streets.

'And too young, my dear, hardly out of nappies…'

'Coming down on us like that, phew, wanting to shut down Senstar…'

'We might have listened to him then.'

Questions were asked between the white walls of the swan houses. 'Has anybody seen these test results he's going on about? '

'Why, no,' heads were then shaken with disgust. 'And why should we bother with his fabrications? It's all a ruse to put a stopper in our exports to the sea coast.'

'Or get himself promoted at his job.'

All the while, in his bakery, Alex Sage was following his own line of investigation.

'Hello, Mrs Lavender, how are you today?' he would greet his regular morning customer. 'Will you be having the usual? Two poppy seeds loaves'.

He would wrap the freshly baked, mouth-watering goods in brown paper. Then his ball-round body would roll a few steps and lean over the wooden counter. The watery blue eyes would have a knowing, conspiratorial look in them and the bulging cheeks would pink with exertion.

'Did you know what that louse has been up to all this time? A bird told me, a very reliable bird, mind, that he's been snooping for days around Senstar, asking questions. So, I'm thinking, why, why would he do that? He's been trying to steal the secret recipe for our chocolates: that's why!'

The days eloquently turned into weeks, the weeks-into a month. Stellaria burned in the flames of righteous anger. There was nothing like the common threat to the reputation of the town to forge the tightest of bonds between its citizens. Not long ago, some of them had been assassinating each other daily with rapiers of sharpened wit.

Arc Libertia, however, had never stopped. Now in his 10th year of orating, he couldn't remember a time when he'd lost a single verbal battle. This morning, leaning casually on the wall by the wrought-iron school gates, he was scanning the faces of the passing 'midgets', contemplating his next victory.

There it was. He moved swiftly, with that ease that predators have, to block the path of a tensed, dark-haired boy.

'Mark,' Arc cocked his head to one side. His voice was thick with mock concern. 'How is your oration doing these days? Running out of steam I hear? I could give it a nudge, you know: if your miniature brain cells can stomach it. Ouch, they look like they are ready to fall apart at as much as a puff of brilliance.'

Arc's laugh resonated loudly in the school yard. Mark lifted his eyes off the tips of his black school shoes and shot a single, dark look of loathing in his direction. He then scurried to the relative safety of the classrooms beyond the gate. Like so many others like him he thought that swallowing his pride would hurt less than being humiliated in a public battle of wits. Nobody could outspeak Arc–nobody. That was a fact as hard as they came. Hard enough to squash any town's memories of what Arc had been in his first year at the school: the older kids' oration punch bag. Well, he had soon turned the tables on them. He had discovered that you didn't need to be that smart to outsmart others. All it took was being… vociferously cruel.

Erie was not far behind Mark when it happened. She witnessed Arc's feat with her heart in her throat and feet glued to the cobbled stones underneath. Getting near the school entrance, she prayed not to be the next target. But then…

'Well, well! What have we got here?' Arc whipped around at her. Hands over his hips, he positioned himself on her left. Ray, his lapdog, stood on the right.

'A stinking traitor! With a fish- guts stench!' Ray made a disgusted grimace and pinched his nose. 'That's the traitor that obviously, doesn't care enough about our town to say a *single word* against that science-squirting worm! '

If it had been any other day Erie would have taken the blow silently. Like Mark. Like any sane person would have done. But now, in the space of a few heartbeats, the years of anger and humiliation heated dangerously red inside her. The lava- filled volcano could take no more of that safe silence, of escaping, of keeping the appearance of being like everybody else. The truth was that she wasn't a true Stellarian and was never going to be. She'd been a ridiculously black sheep amongst a flock of white swans since the day she was born.

'And do *you* care that we're all being poisoned? Erie's voice came out low, through gritted teeth, but picked up more force with each word. 'Do you imagine that some oration geniuses will deliver a few dazzling speeches and save the day? You are wrong! Speeches won't help if our livers shut down because of toxins.'

'It couldn't possibly be that serious, it's just…' Erie's fierceness took Arc by surprise. But only for a moment. His prowess on the oration field kicked in and he started gathering his thoughts.

At that moment perfectly styled blond waves floated into Erie's vision.

'Aw, the mangy kitten's got some claws! How adorable!' Nicole taunted. Folding her left arm, she propped her right one over it and placed a glittery, pink-nailed finger on her chin. Her violet-blue stare as she met Erie's, was cruel and amused. Then a cold, silvery laugh tinkled out of her lips. A crowd started gathering around, anticipating a good show.

'Not serious, Arc? ' Erie asked undeterred. 'Science proves itself by tests unlike oration. Mr Lewelin and his team have done these tests. The pesticide concentration in the cocoa is higher than the safe limit, that's a fact. Three times higher! And if you're thinking,' Erie parried Arc's snicker, 'of saying now that these limits are some wishy-washy hogwash, save your breath! Scientists all over the world have studied pesticide residues for years, for decades actually, ever since the book *Silent Spring* showed how dangerous they could be.'

'Well, I agree with that,' Arc's conceded with a suave smile, 'they *could* be dangerous. But the question is: dangerous for whom exactly?' His Grecian-sculpted face under the waves of blond hair and the calculating grey eyes left no doubt that the King was back in control. 'For us… or for these scientists that would lose their jobs if they don't discover a grand environmental threat? What better way to keep their research money flowing in than raising the alarm in all the chocolate factories in the country? There are tests to be carried out overseas too-on the pesticide doses in the cocoa plantations. And let's not forget the poor aquatic wriggly creatures, they have to be saved too! The list goes on and on.'

The King of oration looked around the swelling ranks of pupils gathering at the school gate to witness his triumph. He made a smooth 'she's going dooown' move with his right hand. Nicole laughed cattishly. Some Year 10 boys whooped it up:

'Go, Arc, go!'

'Give her a good grilling, Arc!' Ray joined in.

'Just wait and see!' Arc's eyes flashed victoriously.' She will be in heap of snivels before the bell rings!'

But Erie had no intention of surrendering, not today.

'Do you know that the Expert Committee on Pesticide Residue in Food tests more than 3000 samples of food in the UK each year? And that trading standards, MRLs, are set for the whole of Europe! This is because all these countries work hard to have clean, safe food. If it was just one big scientific gimmick, would millions of people support it? Or are you prepared for Stellaria to become the next scientific proof of pesticide toxicity?'

'Oh, prophet of doom, spare us!' exclaimed Arc dramatically and everybody around him and Erie laughed. But it was an uneasy, quiet laugh this time.

‘Why didn’t you, or you, or you’, Erie pointed at Arc and each of his cronies, ‘ask about Mr Lewelin’s test results? Why didn’t you bother to do a little digging? I did. Our chocolate is pretty nasty spiced with endosulfan. Before the ban in 2011, cashew crops in Kerala, India were sprayed with this pesticide. So, thousands of people suffered from physical and mental disorders because of it. Babies were born with deformities too. ’

Arc had been expecting a swift victory. He found himself having a growing morsel of respect for Erie’s stance. But this didn’t mean he would acknowledge it.

‘If you do a little more of that ‘digging’ of yours, the erudite word for which is ‘research’, by the way, you’ll be enlightened, let hope, as to the complexity of scientific testing! Scientific results are dependent on a large set of variables specific to the conditions of the study, including its location. For that reason standards, like MRLs, are far removed from being universal.’

‘Well, what about a ban on endosulfan in 127 countries? Is that universal enough for you?’ Erie was pleased to see Ray’s smirk freeze half way up his face. The school bell rang shrilly in the brief silence.

‘We’ll continue this another time,’ Arc growled, his stare leaking venom into Erie. He turned his back to her and walked off. *This girl simply didn't want to let go!* Balling up his hands into fists, Arc thought, for the first time in his life, that he had left a battle unfinished. A battle not won.

Two Necklace Hills away, at the time when the school bell put an end to the oration explosion at the school, Mr Lewelin was considering an exit from his own battle. He was oblivious, of course, to the fact that a single Stellarian had dared come to his defence. It was human nature after all, he thought, and therefore Stellarian, to be in denial. He had come to this remote town, at first, secretly hoping to prove himself wrong. Samples after samples were taken personally by him to the lab in London, followed by painstaking analyses. In his profession there was no room for mistakes: businesses, even people's lives depended on the results that the lab equipment churned out. So the scientist had checked and rechecked. All the samples from the chocolate factory had been contaminated with dangerous amounts of pesticides. Full stop.

Mr Lewelin had contemplated returning to London, of course, much sooner. Nobody would have blamed him if he had, if had gone back to his lab and his modern, gadget-filled flat by the Thames River. But he felt something was missing, a piece of the puzzle. So, he stayed on in Stellaria. He had tried to explain that environmental disasters are not always evident, in your face, like a spill of petroleum in the Gulf of Mexico. Sometimes they happened in a hidden, scarier way. Poison trickled slowly through the food chain, month after month, year after year, piled up in the tissues of animals and humans. If left unchecked, one day it could very well cripple entire populations. Or towns gorging on chocolate.

But all his efforts had been to no avail. *Nothing more to be done here*, he thought. Stellarians *were* an odd bunch indeed. They lived in the Scottish Highlands but spoke neither English nor Scottish. Theirs was some kind of an oration language, with illogical logic…Facts couldn't convince them at all.

That morning Mr Lewelin finally decided he'd have enough. Packing his few personal belongings didn't take long. Wrapped in his warm parka, he stepped outside Mrs Lavender's house, where he'd taken lodgings, and got into the lab's sturdy four-wheel drive. He turned the key in the ignition. Without any regrets, without any goodbyes, the scientist began the steep descent down the Stellar River Gorge.

Chapter 5
Snow Siege

Up the gorge, fanning over the seven Necklace Hills, an icy cold wind arrived on the wings of dusk. It blew harder and harder. It hurled squalls of gusty snow relentlessly upon Stellaria, robbing the night of gleaming stars. In a single night, with ferociousness never seen before, the wind gripped the town in a menacing snow siege.

The Stellar River froze over solid.

The path along its bank disappeared from view, sinking into a white grave. The air filled with sharp snowflakes forming chainmail barriers all around the swan houses, swishing, slashing, and blinding anybody who dared venture outside.

In the fuzzy-white morning light John Sylvester drew open the curtains over his bedroom window. He jerked backwards as a huge spruce toppled over on the other side of the glass, crashing to the ground with deafening noise and a blast of snow dust.

A troubled crease furrowed the mayor's forehead. Emergencies were his responsibility but he didn't know how to even begin dealing with this one. He was out of his depth, mentally and physically, unable even to go out of his house in the four-foot deep snow.

He thought about putting together a schedule for clearing at least the main streets. Will the phone lines work? He went downstairs to the living room and picked up the receiver: no sound. The black phone lying in the corner of the bookcase was suddenly mute. For the first time in his 43 years John Sylvester wished Stellaria didn't have a special, heritage-town status. He wished it was more like the cities, sprawled in the lowland, beyond the mountain range, with their mobiles and WI-FI that wouldn't be down in weather like this. The cities that would have something more sophisticated than shovels for clearing up masses of snow.

He strode to the window on the other side of the room, his eyes following the cruel dance of the snowflakes behind the curved glass. Even if he did get the schedule ready, even if they managed to open up some of the streets, the weather would soon make fools out of all of them. Just a couple of hours more and the streets would be buried again. The skies seemed to have an inexhaustible supply of the blasted white stuff!

'At least we have plenty of drinking water! We can melt the snow on the stove,' his wife jested.

Her poised figure appeared at the entrance to the sitting room. Karen Sylvester exuded the air of a person with whom you felt safe in the scariest of storms.

'John, why don't you come to the kitchen for a cup of tea and some apple strudel? Then we can have a think, come up with ideas of what to do next.'

The 'we' of her words grated badly on his ear. The time when he'd thought his wife a prudent, cable woman was now a fading memory in the mayor's mind, a memory he wasn't even sure had ever been true. Had he valued the opinion of that woman before? What nonsense. Life was a *nonsense* made of stupid, silly little stuff. Silly little conversations! Silly witless morons that didn't have a clue what to do between their apple strudels for breakfast and their beef stews for dinner!

Anger rose like acid in John Sylvester's insides.

'That strudel can go down the deepest rotten snow drift, for all I care!' He jerked Karen's hand away, whipped around, glowering at her. 'Think about what, ah? Ideas for what? Fixing wires with JOKES?'

John Sylvester stormed out of the room. His temper was quickly escalating to a full blown, twisting and roaring tornado of rage. Somewhere in a tiny portion of his mind, some rationally remained, telling him to search for a release. For something to pour the anger into. *Go down. Down the corridor. The store cupboard under the stairs. The shovel-there, in the heap of forgotten gardening tools. Yank it out!* The mayor covered the few steps to the front door with the speed of a wild animal. He wrenched the door open and attacked.

He trusted, and stabbed, and smashed. Reaching up to his chest, the snow pressed on all sides. The shovel fought against it with a vengeance. The morning sun climbed frozenly above the horizon, hazy behind the curtain of falling whiteness. When John Sylvester finally came to a stop, he found himself near his closest neighbour Heath Penstemon's house. A narrow, tunnel-like path stretched behind him grudgingly conceded by the snow.

'Mayor, that's a fine job you've done! Clear a little bit more, will you, up to my door?' Heath's grin was wide behind the crack-opened second floor window. He had very little time to revel in the thought that for the first time he didn't have to act politely with the old crock, before something whizzed in the air. The shovel smashed through the window and flew into the sleepy bedroom, inches away from Heath's head.

Like shards of broken glass the snowflakes continued their relentless downpour over the town. Stabbing with cold, mocking the furry coats, they reeled over the increasingly bad tempers of men trying to open up passageways.

They blew over Philius Sento wedged up to his waist in a snow-drift, yelling at the messenger boy: 'GET PEOPLE TO CLEAR THE PATH! NO-O-OW! '

Over Mrs Lavender, the gossip queen bee, in a red robe at her doorstep, screaming abuse. Her words, picked up by the mountain echo, rose high in the air and rang repeatedly amongst the seven Necklace Hills:

'You, clueless pierrot-rot-rot...you call yourself a mayor-er-er-er...you, good for nothing old prude-rude-rude...Are you waiting for us to starve to death, to freeze in our beds?-eds-eds-eds... '

Over Senstar, over the school to be kept by the snow squalls empty and mute. Over shrieking, backbiting and bickering that juggled the ball of blame from a neighbour to a neighbour, from a husband to a wife, from a parent to a child...Stellaria was held prisoner for seven long days before the snowfall subsided and allowed the streets to be, finally, negotiable.

Monday morning was spent in frustratingly slow opening of pathways. It started with men and women digging the snow from around their homes and then going on to clear the streets that led to the school, Senstar and the Town Hall.

The hours of being out there in the freezing cold, shovelling the cursed snow did nothing to improve the mayor's already dangerously torn mood. The Town Hall clock was gravely measuring the tenth hour when he entered the double wooden doors below it. His face was glistening with frost; his steps up the stone staircase were slow, stiff and menacing.

'Mrs Flax, summon the deputy mayor and all the clerks here!' the mayor ordered. 'Immediately!'

His words startled the tired-looking, middle-aged woman sitting behind a desk. When she looked up her body seized up with fear. This new mayor was an alien, evil creature. The secretary thought better than asking him about the reason for the unscheduled meeting.

'Yes…yes, sir, everybody will be here in only a couple of minutes.'

Short, anxious words and steps followed, hurrying through open doors. They were here now, in the mayor's office: twelve men and women constrained between the walls of the wood-panelled room, standing still in ominous, tense air.

John Sylvester was unrecognisable opposite them, looming over his desk with cold ire coursing through his whole body.

'Sedum!' The words were roaring, flesh-slicing talons. 'The phone lines?'

'Sir,' the young clerk in charge of communications recoiled. 'The river gorge is still impassable, sir. I can't…I have no way of getting a word to the technicians in the city…'

'You can't! YOU CAN'T!' bellowed the mayor. His right fist trashed down the desk like a four-inch hammer. 'FIND a way, Sedum! Get down on your knees and crawl down that gorge, for all I care! Or I'll find somebody with a little more brains to do it!'

The mayor swung sharply to his left. 'Silene, where is the inventory for the winter reserves? Meat, flour, fire wood, ration them for a month!'

'Sir, we-we've planned the reserves based on the last winter's bad spell. It was only two-two weeks of bad weather and not-not as bad as now…'

'You should have planned better then, Silene, shouldn't you?' Sylvester whipped back at the white-haired clerk with malice that could no longer be contained. If only there had been somebody capable, somebody who could take action, make things happen! Instead, the weak, cringing faces of the people in front of him made the floodgates of Sylvester's rage break down violently.

'Get out of here,' he shrieked, 'GET OUT! YOU, CRETINS! Sort out the sorry mess that you call your jobs! And you, Libertia' he pointed an accusatory finger at the deputy mayor, 'YOU'D BETTER SEE THAT THEY DO!'

Eric Libertia considered briefly the wisdom behind the staff's almost frantic scrambling for the door, out of the mayor's reach. There was hardly any point in reasoning with a person who had little reason left inside. Yet, the situation in Stellaria was dire. They had no communication with the outside world. No traders had been able to bring fresh supplies of food through the snow blockade. The electricity cables had snapped in the first days of the snow storm and had been damaged ever since. Candles? How long would they last?

'Mr Sylvester, if I may,' Eric Libertia took a few, cautious steps towards the mayor's desk. All his co-workers had already left the room. 'I- we- believe that help from the city is on the way, now that the tempestuous weather has finally given us a respite. Somebody is bound to reach us soon- either by helicopter, or snow machines and when that happens we'll need to be ready with our emergency plan-'

'Don't speak to me about plans, Libertia! Enough talking, enough pen-pushing, enough dilly-dallying! I want to see results! RIGHT NOW!'

'Yes, sir, 'Liberia began speaking rapidly in an attempt to get the words out before the next vicious outburst from the mayor. 'If you could authorise a survey of household consumption-so we know what amount of supplies will be needed…' The torrent of abuse that followed threatened to suffuse Eric with a permanent loathing for the mayor. But then it all was drowned out by the powerful sound of rotary blades. A helicopter had just landed in the square in front of the Town Hall.

Chapter 6

Killer Instincts

I wasn't looking forward to going back to school. During the blizzard I had stayed at home with my parents and my craft hobbies, experiencing a rare sense of inner warmth, of …tranquillity. Something had started to grow inside me, like an unlikely pearl inside a mud-swathed clam.

The snow path led me from the fourth Necklace Hill onto the foot of the fifth. I noticed Ray Sento and Arc Libertia in their usual, kingly places. They were toying with a younger boy in front of the school gates. Tormenting him until fully satisfied that the message of their undisputed rule had sunk deeply.

Many a time before their bullying had sent icy shivers down my spine. Made me cringe, thankful that some other kid was being tortured and not me. But now…my head felt strangely calm and silent as I approached the school. There was no fear, no urge to escape. If I hadn't known better I would have said that a confrontation could be actually fun.

'The Queen of Dullness, herself!' Ray Sento moved swiftly in front of me. He made an exaggerated sweep with his right hand, stooping slightly in a mocking bow. 'Shall we be taken today to new heights of insipid blether, Your Majesty?'

His gangly body straightened up and his precipice-deep black eyes drilled into mine.

'No, Ray, she's come to give us some more of appalling stutter! And what is that stench? ' Smug, stocky, more muscled but equally tall, Arc leaned over me. 'Is that the rotting corpse of your assignment, Erie?'

'That's,' I snapped, 'the stink of your blood-sucking ego, Arc! How many kids have you humiliated, just to feel good about yourself? Huh? I bet a word like 'humanity' isn't even in your dictionary, is it?'

Arc's face froze with the sheer shock of hearing that. He must have imagined his comeback–after our 'little debate' on the poisoning–in much more glorious light. He didn't expect me to fight back, did he? Not in a million years!

'And don't you come at me with your word juggling again! It will do as much good as your father's speeches have done since the storms began, as much as anybody's nonsense at the Town Hall! Will talking open the road down the gorge? Fix our broken phone lines? Answer me that!'

Arc's eyes narrowed warningly at the mention of his father. There was a dark undercurrent behind the injured family pride, the meaning of which I couldn't read.

'It will do all of these things and more! Once the city officials get here we'll *persuade* them that our town is a priority and resources must be poured in ASAP. Do you have any idea, you mute moron, how impossible it is to arrange for emergency funding from the City, when it is so self-absorbed with its high-cost, high-tech style? Money doesn't grow on trees, but eloquence could make it land on all the right branches. Our branches, you toad-ugly twit.'

'If we hadn't been so obsessed with oration,' I barked, infuriated with his self-righteousness, 'we wouldn't stoop to begging the city for help in the first place! We should have trained technicians amongst ourselves, stocked adequately on food and fuel supplies. Or at least we should have done something about snowmobiles and radio connection!'

Beside Arc, Ray gave out a snort of laughter. 'Mother Nature has gone wild; nobody can escape a disaster now and then!'

'But we could have prepared better for this one instead of whinging and waiting for somebody to rescue us! And where is the City's help anyway?'

Out of nowhere, an arm pulled me, dragging me urgently, away and inside the school building. Jay.

'Stay away from my brother, Erie!' she said, an earnest plea in her voice. 'There is no telling what he can do to you now, after the horrible week we had at home. My dad was…hard on him, on all of us.'

'Are you warning me, Jay? I'm not supposed to be worthy of such effort, remember?' Shaking my head as though scattering away the remains of my fears, I continued. 'Besides, I'm not frightened. Not anymore. Maybe,' I smiled wryly, 'I could surprise him, and you, some day.'

'What do you –'

Jay's question was cut short by a figure crossing the courtyard, moving towards us. It was Ms Dahlia, our English teacher.

'Girls, I expect you not to be late for your class,' she said sternly.

'Yes, miss.' Jay whispered 'Talk to you later,' and we scurried towards our classroom in the Burns corridor.

Our school is a rectangular white building surrounding a fountain courtyard. Its four corridors with classrooms were named after famous Scottish people: Carnegie, Witherspoon, Smith and Burns.

Andrew Carnegie, my favourite, had been a philanthropist who made a fortune from steel factories in America. He'd used his fortune to establish schools, universities, libraries and museums around the world. Our Carnegie corridor houses the infants and the juniors. Its six classrooms, as many as in the Witherspoon corridor, overlook the primary school playground and the school gates beyond.

John Witherspoon, a Church of Scotland minister, was invited to become president of Princeton College in 1768. He went on to transform it into a prestigious school at the level of Harvard and Yale, educating the future leaders of America.

The shorter sides of the school building, the Burns and the Smith corridors have four classrooms each. Of the four historical figures Adam Smith is, I suspect, closest to the hearts of our school governors. He actually delivered public lectures on rhetoric (yes, *rhetoric!*) in the 1750 s. In history though he's better known as the father of modern economy; his portrait was even printed on the Bank of England banknotes.

The Burns corridor, towards which Jay and I were heading this morning, was named of course after Robert Burns, the national poet of Scotland and voted the greatest Scott in 2009.

In class my thoughts wandered off as soon as Mrs Dahlia started discussing the power of persuasion in Charles Dickens' *Old Curiosity Shop.*

Strangely, I hadn't read the book yet. The feeling that I wasn't in a hurry to read it was even more bizarre.

Half way into the dreaded lesson a loud, swishing sound buzzed the room into action. Boys and girls were now all jumping up from their desks and clambering behind the glass, rubbing the condensation film off with their hands. Excited shouts cartwheeled on top of each other and my usually so well behaved classmates were now shoving each other for a better view. Mrs Dahlia joined the din herself, peering outside with as much wild enthusiasm as the rest of us.

It was good news. Great news! The first news we had in a week of horrifying snow gales. A camouflage-painted military chopper had now landed in the town square. Our classroom afforded a perfect view of the men in fluorescent jackets climbing out of it, unloading boxes. So, the City's help had arrived after all.

'A glorious day! A blissful jubilation! A herald of the days when Stellaria will be, once again under the governance of its citizens!' Mrs Dahlia ranted. 'I believe in these extraordinary circumstances we can interrupt our lessons and express our gratitude to the men that have braved the tempestuous elements to come to our rescue! Class, follow me!'

I stifled an amused snort, from my place close to the window's edge, and looked around for Jay. So, behind all the airs she put on, Mrs Dahlia was just another hungry, haggard woman wanting to grab a share of the city's food supplies.

'What do you think they've brought?' Jay asked cheerfully, appearing from the melee of students squeezing through the classroom door. 'And why aren't you breaking your neck to go out like the rest of us? To 'express your gratitude'?'

We burst out laughing. We laughed until there was hardly any air left in our lungs. 'I'm glad you can appreciate oration from the right angle, Jay. The funny one. Let's go,' I said finally, setting off for the cloakroom. 'But I'm not really a big fan of stampedes.'

All the doors along the corridor were wide open; the last remaining students were milling out of the cloakroom as we got in. Jay put on her red cashmere coat, and I -my blue jacket.

'Whatever is in that chopper, it's bound to be better than eating potatoes for four days,' Jay said. She scowled. 'That's what mum's been cooking at home, anyway. You won't believe the week we've had.'

'Was it *that* bad?' I asked quietly. Her suddenly serious eyes were remembering something beyond the mundane diet of the last week, something that had hurt her- deeply. I wished it hadn't been this way. I wished she could have had my seven blissful days, painting the snow-covered Necklace Hills and decorating my bedroom wall with paper roses. Rummaging with Mum in the pansy, going over–sort of rationing– the linen sacks of flour, the apples, wrapped in brown paper and arranged neatly in crates, the flat sausages hanging on strings from the ceiling, and the jars of pickles and strawberry jam. I'd enjoyed helping Mum during the summer months with all of these. As many summers before, we'd made our own, delicious home food in preparation for the snowy months ahead. We'd kept that good old Stellarian tradition going. But nowadays very few Stellarians bothered to stock up for the winter this way; most of the town had come to depend- too much I thought, on the traders. They came every week, laden with fruit, and veg, and fish, and meat to sell at our Saturday Market, then went back, their vans full of rainbow chocolates. That was all good and well- until the snow storms had chained us in. For days eagles hadn't been flying past the Stellar Gorge, let alone traders. And I had the gnawing suspicion that the brief respite we were now having wasn't going to last for long.

'My dad hasn't been himself,' Jay said, while we were walking down the snow path to the Town

Square. Our steps fell in unhurried unison; we weren't in any rush to get there. Whatever supplies had arrived, they weren't going to be just handed out as Christmas presents. The mayor would take charge and distribute them, let's hope fairly. I'd heard that he'd been in the foulest of moods these last few days.

'Let me guess: shouting a lot?'

'Just being plain horrid,' Jay confessed. 'You're not going to tell anyone, are you?'

I managed a self-deprecating smile. 'You're talking to a social outcast here, did you forget? Even if I was bursting with desire to gossip, which I am not, nobody will bother listening to me.'

'Perfect for keeping secrets...'

Saddened, Jay walked in silence for a few minutes.

'Isn't strange,' she mused then, 'how meanness spreads, like the flu, from person to person? I've been hearing all these stories: the mayor throwing his shovel at Mr Penstemon, Mrs Phlox and Mr Sage having a go at each other in the sweet shop. Dad...dad called Arc 'useless blabber' and he said that I'll win the Golden Muse when the judges' brains are all ladled out.'

I couldn't help but give out a chuckle. 'That can actually be a very good thing. The brain ladling part,' I explained, seeing that Jay was nettled. 'You can't imagine how many times I wished that all the judges were struck by some ghastly disease that will keep them in bed all summer. And keep me from going anywhere near the stage of the Golden Muse.'

'You must be afraid of entering!' Jay turned towards me and scrutinised my face with astonishment. 'I've been dreaming of beating Arc at it ever since he won the school's first prize in Year 7! He and Ray have taken gold and silver three years in a row now, it's time somebody changed that.'

'Hmm, I'll give anything to see Arc and Ray beaten at their own game. And by a girl, no less!'

The path shielded by snow-dressed spruces opened into the Town Square and we witnessed the most incredible of sights.

The chopper' landing site was a pandemonium of unhinged, shoving and screaming bodies. Mrs Dahlia was in the centre of it, cursing and fighting a man over a large cardboard box. One of the Year 3s was making away with another box chased by soldiers in fluorescent jackets. The rest of the supplies, unloaded from the chopper, lay in disarray in the snow and pupils, my classmates amongst them, were tearing them open and grabbing the contents.

‘Cans of tuna!’ shouted someone victoriously and started stuffing his pockets.

‘Baked beans!’

‘Sugar!

‘Mince pies!’

The Town Hall staff seemed to be all there. But they weren’t stopping the ruckus, they were fuelling it up! They were joining the most shameful of brawls! I shut my eyes and then opened them again as though to wake up from a nightmare. The Mayor was viciously kicking a girl from my class, who had fallen on the ground. He was swearing, pulling a half-ripped cardboard box off her.

‘Jay, they’ve all gone mad! I yelled.

Jay looked at me with panicked eyes. ‘What are we going to do?’

My mind went temporary blank and then I yelled again:

‘The constabulary! Mr Heather!’

Grabbing hold of Jay’s hand, we rushed across the square, up the path meandering between the fifth and the first Necklace Hills. My thoughts entangled in themselves like a ruffled ball of yarn. The more I ran, the more the ball tied into knots, grew larger, sinister, and then rolled down my legs to trip me over. I finally stopped, gasping for breath.

‘Do you think he’ll be able to do anything at all?’ Jay asked the question that was stuck in my throat.

‘I honestly don’t know.’ I rasped. ‘But it’s the only thing we can do.’

Mr Heather only shrugged his beefy shoulders behind his desk. He looked at us with pity. ‘I’ve got plenty on my hands, plenty. My aides got the brilliant idea to make punch bags out of each other- there, see?’ he pointed to the back of the room. The iron bars of the couple of cells were smeared with still crimson red. And on the inside there were the wrong people: not the criminals, but the police. ‘I had to send for Doc and keep these four from finishing the job: smashing more bones, that is, and pulverising their brains. So, my advice is: look out for yourselves, girls. It’s a jungle out there,’ he guffawed, ‘a snow jungle.’

Chapter 7
A Birthday

The following days up to the end of December couldn't have been stranger and more confusing. Stellaria was nothing short of a town that had gone around the bend and fallen down some dead vertical mountain cliffs.

Nobody bothered to go back to school after the rampage at the Town Square. Neither of the teachers attempted to pull us back into the cobweb of education. That afternoon Jay and I had decided that the safest thing to do was to head straight home from the constabulary. So, we'd parted wishing each other good luck with whatever madness we were about to deal with from now on.

Anxious, Mum met me outside our house and hugged me tightly.

'Erie, thanks God!' she gasped. 'I've been worried out of my mind! Mrs Lavender came all the way to the factory, raving about choppers, and boxes and brawls at the Town Square. What happened at school, Erie? Are you alright?'

'It was awful, mum, truly awful. Jay and I ran to call the constable but he just, just…'Tears spilled out and poured over my face, over my words, as I told Mum what had happened.

'I don't think anybody could do anything now. It's gone too far. But Erie,' mum pulled away, holding me by the shoulders. She looked at me intently, with great urgency. 'No matter what happens, we must stick together: you, me, and dad. There is no telling what the others might do, but we can always trust each other. Right?'

'Yes,' I nodded. *Yes. If anybody could resist that contagious madness spreading around the town, it was my parents.* They were like an anchor lodged deep into the sea bed. Let's just hope there wasn't going to be an earthquake under the froth-white waves.

Mr Sento had attempted to re-start the production in the morning as the road had just been opened up. But no sooner than the workers arrived, they started clawing at each other like wild cats. They threw punches at everything that came in their way: other workers, moulding trays, boxes of chocolates. By the time Mrs Lavender had come running with the news from the Town Square, Mum said, no less than half of the packing room had been thrashed. Breaking up the fights had proved impossible and at the end, Mr Sento and Mr Thomson had resorted to jostling everyone out and locking the factory doors. Just as well, I thought. No more poisonous chocolates would be made.

While Mum was staying safely at home with me, Dad became unusually busy. That day and in the days to come he was needed to stitch bleeding cuts, bandage broken fingers, arms and ribs, and deal with infected knife wounds. His junior partner, Mr Lee Narcis, was taking half of the cases himself, but both of them were still called all hours of the day and night. The injuries they were seeing were becoming increasingly vicious while the medical supplies brought on the chopper were dwindling at an alarming rate.

My own battle was looming closer. I couldn't pretend anymore that my birthday was far away, or that with all the upturned reality around me, it would somehow fail to arrive. High above the chaos, the Town Hall clock was still ticking away, still measuring the time in the circles of its iron hands. How I wished that these implacable hands skipped the twelfth hour at noon! That the fateful stroke never, never sounded over the swan houses!

Still, it came. The last day of December dawned in the grey, murky light of an overcast sky. A flotilla of snow-laden clouds lay in an illusive calm, just waiting to haul its guns through the portholes and bombard us with masses of white cannon balls. I didn't know how we were going to keep the roads open this time; I didn't know how we were going to survive. But at least, by now, I had a clear image in my head of what I was going to do next.

'Morning, mum.' I entered the warm kitchen, infused with the aroma of baking. Mum had the wood stove going and was whipping the fluffy strawberry cream for my birthday cake.

'Good morning, birthday girl.' She gave me a huge hug. 'You've grown two more inches since yesterday, I swear!'

'I have,' I joined in on the joke, keeping my face straight, 'so now I am tall enough to reach the top shelf and,' my hands caught the tubes of red and white frosting, 'decorate my own 16th cake!'

'Dad and I have been so lucky to have you.' Mum hugged me again; this time her joy was intertwined with worry. 'The town is not what it used to be- nothing is as it used to be–but we love you just the same, Erie. '

I returned her hug. 'Yes, mum, I know. Thank you.'

Mum spread the strawberry cream over the top and the sides of the cake, making it smooth and even. It was beautiful. Baked with cinnamon and walnuts, and raisins, wrapped up in the light as feather cream that I knew mum had almost fought over in Mrs Phlox's sweet shop. I started drawing swirling motifs with the red frosting over it, then white roses. Tracing its edges made me think of another round shape, this one metal and heavy. The Town Hall clock. My chest tightened. The time for breaking my surprising news was drawing nearer.

The staircase creaked under Dad's slippers and in a moment he appeared in the kitchen. Now, my family was complete: mum, dad, and me.

'Happy birthday, my girl!' dad said and took me in his strong hands. 'Are you ready for the big day? Purple scroll and all?'

'Dad, I *am* ready.' Released from the hug, I looked solemnly at him and then at mum.

'But not in the way you expect.'

'What do you mean, Erie?' Dad asked amused, his eyebrows shooting up, his lips parting in a smile. He was expecting some cheerful surprise, I realised, and I was sure to disappoint him.

'I know what it will mean, for all of us, and I really thought hard about it...Mum, Dad,' I steeled myself, 'I'm not going to enter the Golden Muse. There is no purple scroll.'

'You...what?' There was a thud as Dad slumped onto one of the kitchen pine chairs. 'How could this even.... cross.... your mind?'

Mum seemed more composed, but sadness rose up in her eyes. She slowly lowered herself into another chair, and I took the low stool in between them. It felt like I was five years old again and my parents were about to give me a lecture on how important my first school day was going to be. How I had to make sure I loved oration and earned Mrs Zinnia's praise.

Dad shook his head regretfully. 'We could have encouraged you more, bought you more of these oration books. You have the mind for it, the potential. If only you had worked harder at it, you... you could have beaten Libertia's son this year. I had such hopes for it...'

'I am sorry, dad. I really am. But I could never do it. Winning the Golden Muse takes a strong belief in it. But I ...I don't believe in oration.'

Mum and Dad's faces registered pure shock.

'Not in the way our town is obsessed with it. Can't you see? For twenty years we've done nothing but talk and talk. Where are our farms, our craft shops, our orchards? You've told me how creative, how self-sufficient Stellaria was in the past. But now all we can do is starve in the snowstorms and beg the City for help.'

'How *dare* you talk like that?' Dad yelled, outraged. 'ORATION IS WHAT MAKES OUR

TOWN GREAT! UNIQUE!' His whole body shook with emotion. He threw a furious look at mum:

'That's all your fault! You let her read these useless books: fiction, travel, and all that nonsense. They filled her head with cotton floss!'

'And who said to leave her alone, to stop with the tutoring? It wasn't me! *I was* helping her finish all the assignments. Every day! So, don't blame me!'

'You are her mother. You should have taken care of her!'

'And you are her father!'

I jumped up and with my hands outstretched made myself a live barrier between them: 'STOP IT! Blame me all you want but stop fighting each other! Please!'

My parents' faces relaxed a little. But their familiar features were still distorted by the wrangle and I desperately wished that the kindness was let back in. I needed their understanding and support so much…But even more than that I needed them to remain themselves: the best, the most loving parents in the world. The thought of them hurling furniture at each other and shrieking- of losing them to Stellaria's madness, was unbearable. Not mum and dad! The whole town could go to pieces, but not them. *Please, not them!*

'Mum,' I said, keeping my voice calm with a great effort, 'do you remember my favourite bedtime story when I was a little girl? '

A memory flickered in Mum's eyes. They focused quizzically on mine.

'It's about a time when our town was different. When people were different: each one had their own talent. Some were tailors or glass makers, others invented a singing necktie and my favourite-an alarm clock that 'rang' with the aroma of an apple strudel. All workers could wake up thanks to it and go to Senstar on time for the morning shift. Our whole town was the happiest then…when you could follow the path of your own heart. I don't know when and why but we've lost all these different possibilities. Only one remains now: being a great orator…'

'Is that so bad?' Dad asked. 'You earn the respect of the entire town; and there is always the possibility that somebody important from the city will notice you at the Golden Muse, offer you a well-paid job there -when you are older, of course.'

I shook my head. 'How many employers are out there to grab us for our fluency in Aristotelian polemics? I don't know, dad. But in any case that could work out for somebody like Ray or Arc. Somebody born with a love for word battles.'

'And you love stories, and drawing, and flowers,' Mum whispered, quietly as a sigh.

We all stilled. My parents' eyes overflowed with disappointment, with resigned sorrow. My throat constricted painfully, trapping my voice inside. If only I had been able to speak! I would have painted with words the picture that was so vivid in my head.

I was travelling... Visiting the farthest, forgotten corners of the earth... Listening to the pain, to the wisdom of the people there, imprinting the knowledge of it onto the white paper. I have never been able to master the spoken words, but the magic of their written form ran deeply in my soul. Great books could inspire people to fight for their freedom, to persevere, to withstand the most unimaginable hardships and come out victorious. Somehow, deep inside, I knew I could write good books one day, and perhaps even a great one.

'You are who you are,' dad said heavily. The consternation rang clear in his voice. 'Nobody can change that, not even you. But you have to be prepared for what comes next. The whole town will turn against you, and against us. In the past they would have been content to shower us with insults, perhaps ostracise us. Things are out of control now, so much so, that-'

Dad couldn't continue. What would the town do to a girl who broke away with tradition? Who didn't want to enter the most prestigious oration contest?

Mum stood up, gently squeezing my shoulder in silent support. She then turned towards Dad:

'Nicolas, it might not be as bad as we imagine. A missing purple scroll must look trivial to people who're starving, running out of candles and firewood. Most families are on the brink of a disaster themselves; they would hardly come raining vengeance on us. What we need to do now is be here for Erie, no matter what the consequences. We must stand together-as we've always done.'

'Yes, always,' dad said and came over to embrace us both.

Chapter 8: New Beginnings

When the Town Hall clock struck twelve at noon, John Sylvester lifted his head from the report he'd been reading at his desk. It was a depressing task. The report described the dire food shortages, the month-long electricity black out, the riot in the Town Square, the fights and the stabbings. He'd gone over it again and again, and still couldn't bring himself to send the whole sorry mess to the City by a courier. It would mean an admission of failure–his failure as a mayor.

Yet, it could wait for a few more minutes, perhaps a few hours. John Sylvester's sharp memory kept track of all the birthdays of children that were about to turn 16. He expected Erie and her parents to walk through the Town Hall's wooden double doors any second now.

'Mrs Flax, I will be expecting the Bells by the scroll display.' His tone wouldn't have been different, had he been ordering the whole family to be put in handcuffs. His manner was habitually rugged these days, just as the Seven Necklace Hills had turned into the rugged sentries of the snow storms.

The mayor walked out of the office and down the green-carpeted corridor. The ornate scroll cabinet was in an alcove by the eastern wall of the building. It was an embodiment of his greatest achievement: creating the Golden Muse and bringing Stellaria together under the banner of oration. The purple scrolls in the cabinet, tied with silver ribbons, displayed the names of all 16- year-olds who have joined the contest so far.

Suddenly a crease shot through the mayor's forehead like lightning.

Will there be a Golden Muse next summer?

The town was hanging by a thread, just hanging. He was surrounded by imbeciles, all of them. How was he supposed to fix things when nobody in this damn town followed orders? Nobody came up with any sane ideas?

And where were the wretched Bells anyway? It didn't matter that their daughter was a nutcase who'd never win the Golden Muse. Tradition was everything in this town. EVERYTHING!

The mayor strode agitatedly outside. The crisscrossing, footprint-marked lines in the white snow were the only signs of life. The entire town appeared numbed with cold, slipping into a silent death.

Very well, thought the mayor. Their house was a five-minute walk away and he'd be damned if the newly started snowfall was going to stop him.

The snowflakes were falling thin and sparse but still managed to cut into his bare face. The snow underneath his boots kept pulling him in, sinking him into waist-deep pockets. One, two, three, four times he fell through. The icy curtain of fresh snow thickened, pleating itself around the mayor, blinding him with sharp blades. He reduced his eyes to slits against it, cursed and kept moving. By the time he finally made it to the Bell's house his temper had escalated to pure spite against the world- and everyone in it.

The spite went all into the deafening smash of his fist against Erie's front door. BANG! BANG! BANG!

'Cowards!' he yelled. 'Did you think to hide in your warm hole? To forget about your duty? It's your duty to Stellaria, snivelling worms!'

Inside the house Angelina was pleading with Nicolas:

'Leave it for another day, Nicolas, please. We can't trust the mayor now; he wouldn't see any logic or reason. Tomorrow. We'll go to the Town Hall tomorrow and discuss it sensibly.'

'Angel, I hear you but I really think that if I leave the mayor outside like that, it'll only invite more trouble. The neighbours are sure to come and see what the racket's all about. And then the whole town. With a crowd behind him the mayor himself might decide to lynch us, the state he is in.'

'They can't do anything to us if we stay inside, can they?' Erie asked anxiously.

'SHOW YOUR FACE, BELL! OR I'LL–THRASH–THE–DOOR!'

'No, my dear, we'll be safe inside.' Angelina shivered at the savage snarl. She felt the hall doorway tremble under the mayor's wild thumps and her hand enveloped Erie's shoulders protectively. 'Nicolas?'

'It's going to be alright. I'll talk to him outside.'

Nicolas Bell put on his coat and hurriedly, before Angelina could stop him, opened the front door.

He narrowly escaped the mayor's punch that was coming that very second down onto the blue-painted wooden surface. Nicolas's first impulse was to answer that punch with one of his own, but he thought the better of it.

'What the heck are you doing?' he yelled. 'You'll regret this, mayor, if you don't calm down! I'm warning you!'

'Are you, LEECH? And what exactly are you going to do, ha? Hide?' John Sylvester's voice was pure menace. '*I'm warning you*, Nicolas, if I don't see that purple scroll right now, you are all

GONERS! The wrath of the entire town will pour down your pathetic little house!'

It was the last straw. Bell brought his clenched fist down onto the mayor's face and sent him sprawling into the white coldness. 'That's my scroll! And don't you dare! Don't you dare threaten my family, you lunatic!'

The mayor touched his face with one hand and felt something sticky trickling down the stubble of his left cheek. Fire blazed in his eyes. Blazed with such ferocity that not a drop of sanity could survive in it.

He lifted himself up slowly, too slowly. It was a feint to fool Bell into thinking that the mayor was too old and frail for fights. Then he rammed Bell with his whole body into the house front wall. In the next moment the men were a melee of punches and kicks, and guttural panting, rolling into the snow. Bell held Sylvester under him and swung the ball of his fist into the mayor's left ear. The mayor couldn't catch the blow but he caught the next one and then jerked forward to hit Bell in the ribcage. Bones cracked. Bell let go of Sylvester and the mayor was upright now kicking him brutally. Bell managed to trip the older man with his leg. The mayor lost his balance and Bell was on top of him, twisting and pinning his arms down, pressing a knee into Sylvester's lungs until the mayor started struggling for breath.

'Enough! ' Angelina bolted out of the front door. She held a thick piece of wood in her hand but seeing the mayor was on the ground, let go of it.

'Nicolas, you've got to stop this!'

Suddenly shrieking pierced the air like a volley of poisonous darts. It reverberated through the Seven Necklace Hills:

'HE'S KILLING THE MAYOR! HELP! THE BELLS HAVEN'T GOT THE SCROLL! ABOMINABLE CANKERS!'

Angelina's heart began thumping madly inside her. She knew who was screaming even before she looked up at the 'observatory' of their neighbour's house. Mrs Lavender. She was a woman possessed. And they had only minutes left before the end.

'Hurry, Nicolas, hurry! Inside!'

Erie's parents vaulted inside the house. They put the metal bar lock across the front door and started hauling the walnut dinner table towards it.

'Erie, run! Into the cellar!' Angelina shouted.

Erie, who'd seen everything through the living room's window, moved instead towards the large china cabinet in the corner.

'I'll help! Mum, push it on the other side, so we can move it behind the window.'

Both Nicolas and Angelina turned, surprised at the calmness of Erie's voice. Their daughter's face bore no signs of fear. It was determined, like that of a soldier entering a battle. They felt proud of her.

'Do it,' Nicolas said, moving away from the dining table that was well wedged behind the door, 'and then all of us are going down into the cellar.'

The cellar opened through a hatch on the kitchen floor. It was used for keeping jars of compotes, relishes and pickles but in the last month it had been more of a fridge; the real fridge not working with the electricity black out. The square place, bordered with earthen walls, was just big enough for the Bells to fit in. Nicolas lowered the hatch down, chained it on the inside–

The path to the beautiful swan house had never seen so many feet clumping, pounding it down. The vanguard, Philius Sento and Rob Thomson, reached the blue front door and began hacking axes into it. Alex Sage swung his shovel wildly through the sitting room window, spurting glass everywhere. Mrs Lavender appeared next to him, stabbing her metal poker into the white façade. She maimed it with wounds like bullet holes before toppling down the 'Bell Cottage' sign with a cattish laugh. More men and women stormed belligerently up the path. Roaring and screaming threats, they slammed the trunk of a fallen spruce against the china cabinet. Again, and again, and again.

The elegant, curved white walls had taken years to build but now they were bleeding plaster in the matter of minutes. The china cabinet crashed down, leaving a gaping hole in its place. Seconds after, the entrance covered in deep gushes, finally gave in. The entire house shook with despair and the hordes stormed in.

What happened next was.... inexplicable.

Bellflowers burst out of the depths of the earth and twined along the cottage walls. Dozens of them, stretching, elongating their stalks, forming tips that peeled open into more leaves and more flowers. Vivid blue and velvety green, weaving a magical web everywhere.

The Stellarians with crazy eyes halted as if suddenly petrified. Their limbs refused to move. But their minds shifted, started mellowing and surrendering. The powerful force of the flowers was telling them now to let go of anger. To let go of jealousy and compulsion. To be themselves and wide open the gates to their dreams. Happiness streamed beyond these gates in shimmering lights, beckoning. *Be brave*, the force said, *follow the path. Take others as helpers not enemies and you'll reach further than you ever imagined.*

Alex Sage closed his eyes to listen. He listened to this newly found peacefulness in his heart. The world had never felt so purposeful, so blissful. He had *his own* place in it; a place that he could reach without knocking others down on his way. Sage's outstretched hand touched a blue bellflower. His inner eyes saw the true dream of his heart.

Many more hands repeated the gesture. Smiles blossomed on the faces of women and men. They began dropping their weapons, hugging each other and saying what they'd felt. The mayor, who had gone upstairs in a rage to look for the Bells and smash their belongings, now came down and hugged Sento.

'I haven't felt so good in years. Years, Philius! Nothing can stop us now, old chap! We'll have the electricity back on! Clean up all that snow, get Senstar running! Everything's going to be as before! No, I'm telling you, it's going to be BETTER!'

It was then when John Sylvester noticed that there was something wrong with Sento. He was as white as the snow outside; his eyes looked as if they'd seen the black scythe of Death. Next to him Rob Thomson was likewise drained of all colour and unresponsive to the jubilation engulfing the Bells' ground floor.

'Philius, my friend, you look awful! What's the matter with you?'

'Let go of me!' Abruptly, Sento tore away from the mayor, away from the bellflowers blanketing the wall behind. 'Not everyone wants to play the gullible do-gooder here! Few stinking flowers and you start hugging like soppy idiots. Not me! Not me!' he screamed. Followed by Thomson, Sento pushed his way out of the room. Both men took to the path outside almost at a run.

'They're fighting it, the fools,' Mrs Lavender commented, standing by the broken window, shaking her head in pity. 'Sooner or later they'll come to admit the truth, though. Fighting on the wrong side had never done anybody any good.'

For a while John Sylvester looked pensively in the direction of Senstar's director and manager's disappearance. Then a thought flashed in his mind and he started hastily for the kitchen.

'Nicolas, Angelina, Erie, come out!' He called over the cellar hatch. 'Everything is different now. We're not going to harm you.' The mayor looked around, at the smiling faces of people gathering around him. 'There are flowers, bells flowers, all over your place. I honestly don't know what else you can do in a house like this but,' he grinned widely, 'celebrate!'

Chapter 9
Rays of Sunshine

The bellflowers rose up all the way to the topmost room of the house, tuning into the art work on my walls with splashes of blue and green. On the outside they'd also used the white walls like a huge trellis, convoluting up as high as the black roof tiles.

While the mayor was assuring Dad he'd personally see to it that the front door and the window were repaired, mum and I did some investigating. The long bellflower stems led us to the back of the house and into my garden. There were roses out here, tulips, peonies, gold honeysuckles and chrysanthemums, all sleeping under the snow. Why not the bellflowers too? How did they grow, in the dead of winter, to cover our entire house? There was nothing that could help us fathom their magical powers either.

'I'm not sure we'll find any more answers today, Erie,' mum shook her head in bemusement. 'I never thought I'd see flowers covering every spot of white wall, all the way to the chimney, but it looks splendid! Marvellous! These flowers have given us back our dreams, Erie! Can you imagine all the possibilities we've got now?'

Even my imagination didn't prepare me for the squall of plans, handshakes and hugs, and the feverish activity inside our cottage. The people in here were radiating so much enthusiasm that it seemed to melt the very snow chill coming from outside. I could hear scraps of conversation over the din. The baker, Mr Sage was saying something about a library while next to mum, Mrs Phlox was throwing wildly her hands in the air and enthusing about…What was that? 'Petty furore?'

Awed, huddled near the warmth of the fireplace, I looked around the sitting room and listened. After so many years, it had finally happened. IDEAS were rising in the air all around me, like multi-coloured helium balloons. In my mind I could see them glittering above, tugging on their silver threads, reaching higher and higher up. Stellarians came and left, bidding the warmest of farewells…and so the ideas left with them to set off on astonishing adventures into the sky.

By the end of the day the entire town must have passed through our house. Judging by the sincere smiles and the high fives, the bellflowers had worked their magic even on the most sceptical of my classmates. Even on the school seniors! My jaw fell wide open when Arc and Ray came in at about five o'clock to…thank me! The bells, they said, were the most amazing thing that had happened to Stellaria in a long time! Ever! For once, I was inclined to agree with them. I could hardly believe the two hands extended in my direction. Me? Handshake with the school most abominable bullies? Slightly regretting the loss of animosity, I'd proffered my hand as well. The verbal skirmishes between the boys and me had recently begun being enjoyable.

Jay and her parents were one of the last people to arrive. I could see Jay touching the bellflowers next to the broken window and marvelling for a few moments. And then…When she smiled across the room, a smile like the brightest ray of sunshine, I felt the last, lingering shadow of sadness leaving me. For the first time in my life, I felt that I mattered. I had as much right to be here, in this room, in this town, as anybody else because… at long last, I was somebody's true friend.

Over the next few days the town was simmering and boiling with ideas. I breathed deeply the freedom afforded by the school holidays. Though I mostly stayed at home, the news didn't fail to reach me. Jay came to visit in the mornings, bringing reports, each one more spectacular than the previous. Learning it straight from her dad, the deputy mayor, she told me how Mr Sylvester had remembered – Ha! And not too soon! – about the snowmobile. He'd hauled it out of the depths of the Town Hall himself. Then he'd flown down the Stellar Gorge to get help.

On the third day after the mayor's departure Jay's bright 'Morning, Mr Penstemon!' and her excited screams found me in the living room. I was wrapped in a coat and a blanket, painting. Though the curved window in front of me was glassed once again, there was still freezing cold air blowing from the front of the house. Mr Penstemon was fixing a brand new door to its hinges there.

'Erie, Erie! You're not going to believe it!'

Jay's feet kept leaping off the floor as though gravity was approaching zero. 'Dad said that the mayor's pulled it off! The food, tons of it, is flying in tomorrow! And so is an entire team of electricians to fix the power lines!'

'Wow!' I beamed. 'How did he do it? Did he talk the City's officials to death?'

Jay and I doubled over and laughed until tears sprang in our eyes.

'Make–fun–of–it all you want,' Jay said in-between fits of giggles, 'but this is one time–when– oration–comes in– useful!'

'You're absolutely right, Jay,' mum called out from the kitchen. In a moment she appeared in the sitting room, her cooking apron over a thick woollen jumper and blue jeans. 'And that's wonderful news. Perhaps, I would be able to get some flour and make one of my famous apple strudels at last! Or some jam and frangipane tarts,' she inclined her head, thinking, 'or maybe some petit fours! Do you know, Jay, I have these idea– '

'Mum! You've been talking about the patisserie non-stop for three days now!'

'Patisserie!' Jay gasped. 'That's fabulous, Mrs Bell! I'll be your first and most faithful customer! Promise! By the way, cream buns are my favourite!'

'That's going to be my Jay's special,' mum smiled. She turned towards me, a slight reproach in her voice. 'At least I'm not keeping it hush-hush like some people I know.' She was alluding, I guessed, to dad's refusal to tell us about his bellflower dream. All we'd gathered was that he was waiting for the phones to be back on, so he could place some mysterious book orders to the city's library.

Jay was suddenly blushing and shuffling her feet. Mum didn't notice it because she returned to the kitchen to figure out how to cook the pitiful remnants of ingredients left. I patted the chair next to me, motioning Jay to sit down.

She slipped in and looked intently in front of her. My oil landscape was lying on an old white sheet that covered the dining table. Come to think of it, Jay hadn't mentioned her dream either.

'I was meaning to tell you,' she started, 'but…it's so weird. How can I do it when I don't even know how to mix paints?'

'Do what? '

Jay chortled, no doubt picturing something in her head. Her face relaxed; the embarrassment telescoped to a couple of tiny dots in her eyes.

'When I touched the bellflowers…I saw the most unexpected thing. But also the most awesome! So, if I want to do it for real, I'd better start learning right now. Will you teach me?'

'Not a chance,' I teased. 'Not before you tell me what that's about!'

Jay swallowed hard. 'A drawing over the façade of the Town Hall. A white horse flying amongst golden clouds!' She shot me a warning look. 'And don't you dare laugh now!'

I *was* laughing. Painting Pegasus, the Greek mythical horse, all over the Town Hall! I could see it now in my mind: the iridescent white of the creature with open wings, set against the azure and the gold of the sky. No other symbol could fit Stellaria's new dreams more perfectly.

'Aw, Jay, that's the best idea ever! Much less painful too, than orating at the Golden Muse!'

Grinning madly, I reached out for a clean sheet of drawing paper.

'Let's do it! Let's paint your Pegasus, Jay!'

We started out with water colours and the background of clouds and sky. Jay was a natural. I only needed to tell her about the technique and she would use it on the paper in front of her. Mixing colours, painting them, watering down and blending. It felt thrilling to be here, at the smoothly dark walnut table, drawing with Jay. Not being alone anymore. Not struggling to appear a *norma*l, oration-mad Stellarian girl but being myself and being…*normal.* It was a two-sided coin, wasn't it? Normality. It had flipped over and I didn't want to think how easily it could…flip back again. I wanted to bask in it, roll in it as if in a lushly green meadow strewn with poppies. For as long as I could.

Jay and I talked about everything that was happening. With the food shortages, and the electricity, and the vicious tempers flying around, nobody had had much of a Christmas holiday up to now. But people's hopes were getting up. A big celebration was being planned in school with the opening of the new term. There was also a talk about a change in the curriculum! It was driven forward by Nicole's mum, Teresa Gentian, one of the school governors. Apparently, she was a frequent visitor to the Town Hall these days, discussing her proposal with the mayor's deputy- Jay's dad. From what I'd heard of the Gentians, they were extremely rich, snobbish and intimidatingly persuasive, all thanks to massive inheritance from an entrepreneur uncle in the city. I really didn't care much what charms Nicole's mum would unleash, as long as the oration was going to be replaced by some sane subjects. Science, geography and history, art and design...*Keep dreaming, Erie!* Jay and I made the most of our remaining week of holidays. We painted at my house and enjoyed the sunshine illuminating the clear blue skies.

As tempers had mellowed before, the snow now began softening, turning into rivulets. The rivulets streamed into the Stellar River and raced, day by day, to the City. Our evening windows soon shone with electrical light. The phone lines began buzzing with conversations. By the time the City's electricians had completed all repairs, the first snowdrops heralded the arrival of the most brilliant and very early spring.

Chapter 10
The School Governors

John Sylvester circled the white building of the Town Hall. It was purely functional, straight and plain. There was nothing swirling about it. Square, with two rows of windows on each side and a Greek arch supported by two Corinthian pillars at the entrance. Heavy, double oak doors with the Seven Necklace Hills carved into them. Black roof tiles on the slanting roof.

The mayor shook his head. The structure had been pitifully left out of the euphoria of building the swan houses. If the walls couldn't be changed anymore, something else, perhaps, could be done. Colour…colour would be good.

The mayor passed through the double doors and climbed the central staircase to his office. He breathed slowly, deeply, with ease that he couldn't recall having before. Ever since that day at the Bells' house, he'd been free of frustration. One after another, the days came to him beautiful, full of promise.

His first meeting in the morning was with the school governors. Teresa Gentian had come up with an amazing new programme that took a lot of the teaching out of the classroom. There were geography lessons planned: flow and water quality of the Stellar River; effects of global warming on the Scottish Highlands, plant and wild animal' surveys. Arts and sports were finally given the place they deserved. There was hardly a student in that school, the mayor thought, who could run a proper mile- not in terms of oration marathons, anyway.

The mayor had already given his full support to Mrs Gentian. He'd even approached some of his contacts in the City, probing for sponsors and additional funds from the government. The only reason why things weren't moving forward as fast as he would have liked, was the other school governor. And that's why they were having this meeting today. It was going to be an interesting day.

Mr Sento reached the mayor's office to see Mrs Gentian already making her way in. He stared at the back of her black Chanel dress with animosity.

'Good morning, Mrs Gentian, Mr Sento,' the mayor greeted them. 'Please, take a seat.'

The school governors moved their chairs wide apart in front of the mayor's desk. They sat down without looking at each other.

'I have a very impressive list of names here,' John Sylvester tapped on a densely written document on his desk. 'They all signed in favour of the new proposal. The students at the school, their parents, the teachers as well as a few other citizens with concern for education: 402 signatures in total. I believe it will be in the town's best interest if we all agree to go ahead with it.'

'And *I believe* that such an important decision should not be taken in a rush,' said Senstar's director authoritatively. He was used to having things go his way. 'These signatures here...have been they given in full view of all considerations? I am afraid a lot of people may have been swayed by the enthusiasm of Mrs Gentian, and forgotten how much oration has elevated the status of our town. Not to mention the economic boost due to visitors especially arriving here for the Golden Muse.'

'There is nothing in the proposal about changes to the Golden Muse, Mr Sento!' exclaimed Mrs Gentian indignantly. 'The contest will be held annually as it has always been!'

'But all these additional subjects you suggest will leave little space for studying oration!' Sento objected hotly. 'How are we supposed to encourage a talent in the greatest of arts when our children will be hopping on basketball courts and trampling across the hills?'

'Trampling?!' Mrs Gentian was beside herself. She shot out of her seat and began talking fast, swinging her hands wildly with every word. 'They will be learning about sustainability and climate change–the most relevant – '

'Governors, we need to discuss this calmly. Must I remind you,' the mayor stared Mr Sento down, 'that manners should be observed in my office at all times?'

The factory's director made an effort to compose himself. 'I do apologise if Mrs Gentian felt offended. This wasn't my intention.' *But I'll do anything to keep the status quo,* he thought. *What that peacock of a woman doesn't understand is that I can mould the town any way I like. As long as I have oration to keep them busy.*

'Might I suggest a town meeting, Mr Mayor,' Mr Sento continued solemnly. 'Before a final decision is made, we owe our citizens a thorough presentation about not only the benefits of the proposal but also *its setbacks.'*

Mrs Gentian's temper burst into crescendo sparks. The sun rays streaming from the window behind the mayor's desk appeared to set alight the waves of her long, silky blonde hair.

'Isn't it time for you, Mr Sento, to *sit back*? To listen to what the town wants? That's what the town wants,' she waved furiously the list of names in Sento's face, 'you unreasonable, old–'

'Mrs Gentian, please, calm down!'

The mayor's voice sounded steady, with a very slight elevation from his usual deep, engaging tone. 'We have already organised two such meetings, Mr Sento. Their result is in front of you: the list of signatures. It speaks louder than any words. The town's decision couldn't have been clearer.'

John Sylvester paused briefly. 'As a mayor I have a duty to endorse all changes that are progressive and beneficial for Stellaria. Opening our educational programme to other subjects than oration is, without a doubt, one of these changes. I must inform you, with due consideration for your objection, Mr Sento, that the curriculum proposal is now in its implementation phase. As from this very moment.'

The mayor gave Mrs Gentian a quick smile before bidding her and Mr Sento good day.

As the door to his office closed behind the governors John Sylvester stretched and exhaled a long, contended 'Aaaah'. *Yes, it was going to be a good day*, he thought to himself. He was determined to make it so, as any other day dawning upon his town. Stellaria was finally going to move forward. No. To take off, to *skyrocket* into the colourful, exciting future. No more of this stale oration, no more of that empty pathos eating at the town's wings.

Whenever the mayor cast his mind back to the events of the last three months, he felt shaken to the very bone. This had been one tough wake up call. First, the shameful speeches all over town which aimed, let's be honest, at making the scientist cringe. Then, the snow siege and the hunger, and the looting. John Sylvester was a rational man. But he couldn't help the feeling, in his gut, that somehow these things were all connected. As the mayor, he should have made sure the debates on the poisoning were handled with due respect, and then he should have gotten the town ready for the coming winter. These were the Scottish Highlands, for goodness sake. What was he expecting? Lounging by the river in swimming trunks, soaking up the January sun? That was exactly the problem with too much oration; it didn't let you actually sit down and think.

On that day when the bellflowers erupted in the Bell's cottage, the mayor made a promise to himself. He had promised himself to seek solutions- not debates about solutions. Together with his wonderful team at the Town Hall, he had been doing just this ever since. And he was going to continue doing it. No question about it.

Unbeknown to him though, there was one solution left untouched. This was because nobody, apart from Erie, realised a problem existed in the first place. Senstar was up and running now, churning out chocolates which Stellaria thought to be delicious and completely risk-free.

Chapter 11 Surprising calculations

I could not believe that spring could come so early to the Highlands. It was the middle of February and I was admiring the tulips in my garden, flaming with red and yellow. There wasn't a single trace of the snow that brought Stellaria down to its knees just a few weeks ago.

I spotted Jay behind the green, wooden fence and waved at her. This morning she came over, so we could go to lessons together. The news I gave her made her feel like she was not just over the moon, but over the entire Milky Way. Hopping, skipping, and practically juddering like a spaceship in the countdown to launch…

'And she said yes, just like that? '

'Just like that! I don't know if it was luck, or a coincidence that I met her that day. Her face didn't look good when she was coming out of the Town Hall, I can tell you that. But then I mentioned Pegasus and she beamed at me, right away.'

'Do you think she can convince the mayor? And help us with the paint?

'Yeah. Definitely. She's really nice, not what I imagined Nicole's mum would be.'

'Erie…' A sudden cloud of worry came over Jay's eyes as we kept walking down the path to the school. 'You know how fairy tale endings are only for fairy tale stories, right? I've been thinking lately that…. a dose of bellflowers, however magical, can't chase all the dark shadows away. What if the winter madness is still here, lingering? What if people start stabbing each other all over again, shrieking and going crazy over a can of baked beans?

There's something brewing in Senstar, my sister tells me. The workers are on their guard against Mr Sento and the manager. And you should be too – with Nicole and her mum. Just because they look friendlier now, it doesn't mean that they can't claw blood out of you.'

My heart skipped a beat. No, the problem wasn't Nicole; I had no illusions about her. But my memory stirred up with scraps of conversations which I heard in the last month: Mum saying that Mr Sento had got rid of his secretary and now stayed cooped up in his office… Ray and Arc speaking in hushed voices; Ray's dad making him do something…

'I can handle Nicole. But Mr Sento is something else. Why did he sack his secretary?

That's a mystery. Senstar is working on full steam now, so he needs her; can afford to pay her, too.'

'Listen, Jay.' I looked into my best friend's eyes, the colour of blue cornflowers. 'Mr Lewelin was right. The pesticides were in our chocolates, they still are. Mr Sento has never given any thought to buying new cocoa. HSE* will have something to say about that.'

'But I thought…'

'You thought it was all talk?'

'Dad told us that there was no real danger. That he'd seen the lab results and they were fine. The scientist, he said, was just too cautious, inexperienced. That was all. The debates at the Town Square were just an excuse to show off our oration skills. I kept out of it, as you know. I thought it was just too much fuss over a little thing. But now…'

'It's not a little thing, trust me. I actually saw the lab reports: Mum had them amongst her papers when she was chairing the Emergency Committee.'

'So, all that time, nobody has taken this thing seriously? Ever?' Mind-boggling, the realisation took a few moments to sink in. 'What are we going to do?'

'I don't know Jay, not yet. But for the moment, I think we should keep our eyes open for anything that doesn't make sense, anything suspicious.'

*HSE:Health and Safety Executive

Later on, in geometry class, I was sitting next to Jay in the second row, trying to concentrate.

Ms Marigold was drawing a larger blue triangle on the board, over a similar but smaller, red one. Her clothes, a flowery tunic matched with black, slightly flared trousers, made her look younger than her forty something years. She turned around and looked at us. I could see humour in her eyes, warmth, and maybe wistfulness.

'…and that's how the huge, aeroplane-view Nazca lines in Peru could have been created. One theory is that, at first, a small picture was made, then from its centre ropes tied to wooden stakes were used to 'blow it up' proportionally in all directions. A very simple method, you see, but the pictures are astounding: a monkey, a hummingbird, a condor, a spider. The largest one is nearly 300 m across.'

My mouth was gaping, I suddenly realised. When it came to painting, I expected maths to be the last thing that could be useful. But it actually was!

'Jay, Jay,' hardly containing the feeling of thrill, I nudged her repeatedly in the elbow. 'We could do the same!'

'Do what?'

'Make the mural to scale, to the size of the Town Hall's wall!'

'You think?' Jay's surprised voice was a loud whisper. She frowned slightly, turning the idea in her head. 'We can't possibly hammer stakes into the façade, can we?'

'Not stakes, but some kind of markers, hmmm, something that we can take off after the picture is finished.'

'Why not ask Ms Marigold?' Jay suggested. 'I've got the feeling that she'll know what to do.'

I lifted my eyes up, wondering if we should do this.

Ms Marigold was looking straight at Jay and me, an intrigued smile on her face.

Strangely, she didn't say a word. In the past, Mrs Zinnia would have poured out a disappointed speech on the lack of concentration in young people and given us an extra oration assignment. Other teachers would have fumed about disrespect and talking over the teacher, then meting out detentions.

Today Ms Marigold chose to simply resume teaching. She had given us a glimpse of what life could be if people didn't squander words. If they handled them as carefully as they would hold gems. Words were as easily devalued as any commodity, as any other too-much-of- good- thing.

Then I imagined words being sold for money. In Stellaria they would have cost pennies in the past, as much as plain lollipops. Today, perhaps, a little more.

'Nicole, why don't you come to the whiteboard and see if you can find out the length of AC?' The teacher's voice pulled me out of my fantasies.

Nicole sauntered from the back of the class. Half-heartedly, she fumbled with a marker:

'Side AC is parallel to that little one here, which is, which is …'

'4cm long,' Mark offered.

'I knew that, of course. Unlike some people, I was thinking,' *Nicole* enunciated the words, '*before speaking*'. She stared him down, hard. 'There is no enjoyment in hearing a previously mute frog croak.'

Mark didn't flinch. 'Well, a frog can sometimes turn into a prince! But what's a fake princess to do? Speechmaking has its limits: it can't change a fake into the real thing.'

A pandemonium-absolute, noisy, and hilarious-erupted! The whole class was doubling over into fits of giggles. Jay and I, and others, leaned over the desks to give Mark high-fives. Some boys even jumped out of their chairs, and were screaming, running madly around the room. But not for long.

'That's enough everyone!' Ms Marigold said with hypnotising authority. She turned to Nicole: 'This is a chance for you to learn how to control your anger, to see beyond your own needs and fears. Why not even turn that anger into a smile?' Ms Marigold glanced appreciatively at Mark. 'I expect you to do exactly that and grow up a little more. Now, back to your seats!'

Such was Ms Marigold's influence over us that for the next half an hour, without any interruption, we did ratios of in similar triangles. I bet that many were still laughing on the inside though. That was such a precious sight to see, an impossible sight, in fact. Nicole had never been humiliated before. Even the girls in her fan group couldn't help smirking secretly.

The bell finally went to release us into the joys of gossip and break time banter. Jay and I stayed behind, fiddling with our rulers and pencils, putting them away in our bags.

'Well, you two must have a question for me?' asked Ms Marigold.

Jay nodded and started hesitantly, 'We have this idea …to paint Pegasus …so the Town Hall looks beautiful…'

'The thing is, Ms Marigold, we want to paint a mural on the façade but we're not sure how to do it. It's going to be huge! Can we do it like the Nazca lines, enlarge it in a similar way?' I finished off.

'That's splendid!' Ms Marigold enthused. 'A mural on the façade? I've always thought the Town Hall looked odd, like the ugly duckling in the Anderson's story. Though, technically it wasn't a duckling at all-it was a young swan and therefore it should have been called a signet,' she snickered.

'Let me think about it...The facade is about 20 metres long and up to the first row of windows, maybe 4 metres high.' Ms Marigold knitted her eyebrows in deliberation. 'And then you've got that Greek style arched entrance right in the middle of it. You might need to do two horses, one on the left of the arch and one on the right, then. What do you think? Two horses, flying towards each other, or perhaps flying away?'

'Not flying away,' Jay said firmly. 'It would look very much like they've turned their backs on each other. The mural should be about something different: about making friends.'

'Beautiful! You'll need a different technique to enlarge it though, girls. The Nazca figures, unlike your mural, are symmetrical. I remember reading about a grid technique which the Italian Renaissance artists used. They painted on a big scale then, in chapels. Let me do some research, first, and maths, and then I'll tell you. How does this sound?'

'Absolutely great,' Jay and I chorused. 'Thank you very much, Ms Marigold.'

On the way to Mrs Dahlia's English we caught up with Mark. Of course, we had to say our cheerful 'congrats' again. It was great to see him, and *hear* him, like this.

'What made you do it?' I asked. 'Take on Nicole?'

Mark shrugged. 'I had something to say, I guess. So, I said it.'

'It sounds so easy when you say it like that.' Jay looked into the distance at something that only she could see. Her thoughts must have drifted back into the past. Or the future's unclear happenings waiting still to take shape? I knew for myself, from my birthday rebellion, that saying what you had to say was anything but easy.

'No matter what, telling the truth is …,' Jay turned her gaze on Mark, 'definitely worthwhile. Take care, Mark.'

Chapter 12
Taking decisions

Nicole was moving away from the school gates, up the cobbled, winding street. Her eyes on the cracks between the stones, she was placing her heeled shoes down very, very carefully. The shoes were a work of art. Custom-made by a specialist in the City, they were silver inside and black outside, with stitches in a mandala pattern.

On occasions when she was sure of her footing, Nicole threw a glance sideways, at the girl walking beside her. She was slim-built, with long, wavy black hair pulled into a ponytail. The nose was straight, proportionate; the eyes–large and catlike. The fair skin glowed healthily, beginning to tan under the unusually warm sun.

Unexpectedly, a realisation struck up inside Nicole like a jolt of electricity. These were no ordinary looks! These *were* the very looks of a popular girl! In fact, with the right attitude, Erie could well be her competitor. On the other hand…Nicole's thoughts were confusing, tearing her in different directions. Some of them were telling her that she should try to make it up to that girl, for all the nasty things she'd said in the past.

Being friends with her, now that she was something of a celebrity, could also come in useful. But for how long was Erie going to stay in peoples' good graces? The new image she'd got now wasn't because of something special she'd done. It was because of the bellflowers. The town was bound to get bored with them soon: what then? Snide contempt will come raining on Erie as it had before. Nicole wouldn't like to be anywhere near the girl when that happened. She'd worked hard, so damn hard, to build a reputation for herself: Nicole, the Queen bee of Year 11. Such a reputation was hardly worth ruining over some sentimentality, or a short-lived benefit…

Today they were going over to Erie's. Nicole's mum had arranged a meeting about the mural painting and she wanted Nicole to be part of it too. What was the point? Painting had never been one of Nicole's interests and that wasn't likely to change now. All she liked doing–all she was good at–was oration. But her mum had insisted. History in the making and all that.

'So the mayor is also coming over to your house, isn't he?' asked Nicole, just to break up the awkward silence.

'Yeah, that's what your mum said, and that he'll have some fantastic news for us. My mum and dad will be there, Jay with her mum and dad, the mayor and you with your mum. I can't wait.'

'It's going to be a great responsibility to paint the Town Hall. You think you are ready for it?' Nicole's tone implied otherwise.

'It's a bit daunting, to be honest. A huge wall to paint and 4 metres above the ground at that. But Jay and I are really excited about it! We'll give it everything we've got. And, judging by what your mum said, we'll get plenty of help too.'

'Not that I think you won't, but something on that scale…Only professional artists would have the experience that such a project needs.'

Erie grinned mischievously, 'But that's exactly the point. We don't have professional artists in Stellaria. We don't have many things other than oration. The mayor's idea is to create something home-grown, something by the town for the town.'

'Well, innovation is always a good thing, I suppose. Still, people are concerned that lately the mayor's departed too much from tradition with his, let's say, flamboyant ventures. A ski resort, orchards, another summer competition overshadowing the Golden Muse. What next?' Nicole pulled a face. 'Building space rockets? I hear Mr Sento is now considered as the more popular choice for a mayor.'

'Considered?' Erie's body tensed. 'By whom?'

‘Oh, I can’t remember names exactly. I’ve been hearing conversations in school. A boy in Year 10 was giving a speech to the primary kids the other day. He’s one of Ray’s friends, I think.’

The mayor’s elections are coming up in May, thought Erie. She couldn’t remember John Sylvester having any competition before, he was so well liked. People respected him. But that, apparently, was about to change. His new ideas were bound to clash with a few self-interests…

As soon as Erie stepped over the threshold of the bellflower house though, her gnawing thoughts dissipated. The ebullient mood inside was contagious. The mayor and Nicolas Bell were talking animatedly on one of the sofas, cheering each other's ideas. Scrumptious treats were laid on a table near them and a dizzying aroma of apple strudel wafted from the kitchen. Mrs Bell followed on its tail.

‘Lovely see you, girls!’ Angelina came up to them and gave each a hug. ‘Welcome to our home, Nicole. Your mum’s on her way, and so is Jay’s family. They’ll be here soon. In the meantime, why don’t you take a seat over there?’ she pointed towards the vacant sofa. ‘I’ve got a few finishing touches to put on the tea feast.’

'And a real feast it is, Angelina! You've got such delights here! These I know, cream buns of course, chocolate cake, croissants. But what are these?' The mayor pointed at small, round pastries arranged on a colourful glass platter. The girls sat down opposite him, getting hungrier by the minute. Nicole, alone, fought the thought of how good all these carbohydrates must taste.

'Petit fours,' smiled Angelina proudly. 'They've got different fillings–ice cream, raspberry jam and these are vanilla cream.'

Nicolas Bell winked at his wife, conspirator-like.

'She should open a patisserie, shouldn't she, John?' he said in a tone suggesting that the idea had just popped in his head.

'Patisserie? You've got the talent for it, Angelina, no doubt about it. I've never been so utterly mesmerised by the smell of apple strudel. In fact,' the mayor briefly considered, 'how would you like it if the patisserie is in the Town Square?'

Angelina gasped. Her whole face lit up and her hands flew towards it, caught in the surprise.

'That's...that's...there are simply no words for it. That will be beyond everything I've imagined!'

Time flew light as a feather from then on. The Gentians, the Bells, the Libertias and the mayor laughed, talked and planned, hardly noticing the hours go by. They talked about artists from the city choosing special outdoor paints and builders coming to smooth over the Town Hall's walls in preparation for the painting. Erie and Jay described the grid method that Ms Marigold had researched for them: first, they would need to divide the A4 picture of Pegasus into 20 equal squares and the façade into the same number of squares but much bigger. Then they could start transferring the painting, square by square, from the paper to the Town Hall's wall. The mayor could already see it all happening in his head. He promised to bring a group of volunteers to help with the grid measurements.

Nicole couldn't remember a time she smiled so much, listened for so long. The bellflowers were doing strange things to her. The more she sat in this room, the more she inhaled their fragrance, the more relaxed she felt. She didn't care what the petit fours would do to her waist; she didn't care about tomorrow's school and defending her reputation. *She didn't care.* These were wonderful people around her, making wonderful plans. She was thoroughly enjoying herself. Without even orating.

Much later that day, lying on the luxurious bed in her own room, Nicole realised how otherworldly the experience had been. In the past she had always been in control, tensed up, ready to pounce like a tigress. She couldn't just let herself go. Her family had a pedigree. Her family was special, coming from a line of extremely successful and influential entrepreneurs. She had to live up to its reputation! Always.

When Nicole was five years old her parents told her that she would win the Golden Muse: every year after her 16th birthday. They furnished the topmost room in the house as a library and told Nicole to study hard. At a time when oration was the make-or-break of social status (as well as money), the Gentians were determined to pursue it with everything they'd got.

Nicole had proven herself a natural leader very early on. The girls in Year One adored her and gave her their toys whenever she asked. The boys fought over who would bring her the school books from the classroom tray. The teachers complimented her on how neat she was and always chose her to carry the register. During playtime, Nicole was always the one to decide what game would be played.

Oration hadn't been that easy. Three years to become a fluent reader. Three more years with the big volumes of speeches in her parents' library:

Demosthenes in Ancient Greece, Cicero in Rome, Abraham Lincoln in America, Napoleon in France and Winston Churchill in Britain.... The old masters had taught her the old-fashioned way. Listening to the oration battles between the secondary school kids had taught her the Stellarian way. By the time it was her turn to move to Year 7 she had done it. She could rally up minds, yes, but also use words as a crooked mirror to bend an argument, or a rapier to pierce your heart. It had been all about power, she realised.

Now Nicole could see a completely different way of life though, a way where other things mattered more than power. The town was changing before her eyes. *Is the old Stellaria better? Or the new one? I'll decide tomorrow,* was the last fuzzy thought before she fell asleep.

Chapter 13
A Bully's Tale

Within a day of the meeting at the Bell's house the mayor had all his team at the Town Hall fired up about the project. Preparations were soon under way for the unveiling of the Pegasus mural at the Spring Party, 12th April.

Ron Silene and Eric Libertia were sent to the city to contact a professional painting firm. Henry Sedum, who had taken some serious screaming from the mayor during the winter siege, was entrusted with the publicity and the volunteer coordination. That was a spot-on appointment because the communications officer was now officially the Town Hall's computer whiz. The moment a brand new computer appeared in his office in the first days of February, Mr Sedum stuck to it like a mouse to cheese. Now, a few weeks later, a few hours on Adobe Illustrator was all it took him to design an eye-catching poster. He was soon out of the Town Hall's doors, clutching a thick bunch of photocopies to distribute around the town. The town square first, then the school, the factory, the swan houses…In no time at all Stellaria was adorned in blue-and-gold posters.

'Exhilarating Art Project in Town!' the posters announced. 'Pegasus to grace the walls of our Town Hall! Are you looking for inspiration? Are you looking for an unforgettable experience? If the answer is 'Yes', come and sign up with us as a volunteer. We'll create an architectural jewel together!'

At the end of lessons Arc was amongst the first pupils spilling out of the classrooms and into the fountain courtyard. The curious new editions to the lunch tables drew his attention immediately. He bent slightly over to read the gold letters, then knitted an eyebrow. The posters were where they shouldn't have been. It was as though they were saying, *I'm here to stay, sandwich crumbs and mayonnaise splodges regardless.*

'A bit too much, isn't it?' muttered Ray. He walked silently from behind Arc and was now reading the poster himself. Other pupils were gathering around the lunch tables nearby, nudging each other, whistling and chatting. 'Don't get me wrong, I like the idea...But 'an architectural jewel'?

'It could well be. Have you seen other buildings with flying horses painted on them?'

'Hmm, not really. But then I haven't seen anything further than Stellaria. So, that's what Pegasus is–a flying horse?'

'Yeah, from Greek mythology. Pegasus was ridden by a hero, who defeated the Chimera monster. The hero and the horse had many adventures together and at the end, Zeus transformed Pegasus into a constellation to stay forever in the night sky.'

'Wow, heroic stuff. Quite catchy.'

Arc thought for a while. 'Pegasus was also a symbol of wisdom in the past. In the 19th century he was considered a source of poetic inspiration. Maybe that's why they've chosen it for the mural.'

'And how do *you* know all that stuff?'

'A school essay. And I liked the constellation stories as a kid.' Arc chuckled. 'Fancied myself a hero, slaying three-headed monsters.'

'Monsters? What's all that negative talk? Pegasus is a beautiful, winged horse, in case you didn't know.' Nicole's shadow glided over the poster in front of them.

Arc observed the girl carefully through narrowed eyes, weighing his choice of words.

'We do know, Nicole,' he finally said. 'We were talking about something else.'

'Oh, alright then. Did you know that the mural was actually my mum's idea? I'll be helping Erie and Jay with the painting. What about you two?'

The boys shared a look. 'Well,' came Ray's non-committal response. 'We might sign up or…not.'

Leaving it at that, Arc and Ray strode across the arched passage, the junior playground and out of the school gates to take up a street weaving between the hills.

'So, we'll give it a try?' asked Ray.

Arc kept on walking, leading the way. He looked at the black dial of his watch. The hands were fluorescent yellow and glowed in the dark. 'It's a quarter to four. The poster said to meet at five at the Town Square. We've got plenty of time.'

'We can go over to my place first. I've got this new thing going, football. Dad would never let me anywhere near it, of course. He switches on the TV only for the debates in Parliament– it's oration in action, that's what he says... I've gotten around it though. I record the match and watch it the next day, after school, when I'm supposed to be doing the Parliament thing. Technically I'm following the rules and watching TV, right? Dad will never know, he doesn't come home until 6. '

'Mate, you are brave!' Arc scoffed. 'Watching football behind daddy's back.'

Ray's grin faded. His mouth set in the stiff line that was a sure sign he was nervous. Keeping silently behind Arc, he let go of the street and climbed up the slope rising to the right. Sparse spruce, rowan and birch trees deepened the grass shade of green here. Only two swan houses dared to stay upright over the steep incline. The third Necklace Hill was the sharpest of them all; it peaked after a short, but heart-quickening walk to unfurl magnificent views of Stellaria and the nearby Glencoe.

Arc chose a group of moss- covered boulders to keep the wind off of their backs and sat down. Ray lowered his lanky body on the grass next to him.

'What are you saying?'

'I'm saying, Ray, that you've got to get your act together. The things that your dad's making you do! The football… well, sneak if you like. But vilifying the mayor, telling people that he's practically off his head! That's *wrong*.'

Ray flinched, 'I just told a couple of people that his ideas are not that traditional. Not that practical really. I might have said that they are far-fetched. And we don't know for sure who got the electricity back, so it might have been Mr Silene after all, not the mayor. A few silly rumours, that's all. Not doing any harm. A bit of healthy competition for the elections, you know.'

This didn't manage to mollify Arc. Sparks of red burst out into his grey eyes like live embers. '*The dotty old bat! Thick as a gang of tortoises playing It?* You call this 'healthy'?'

'That wasn't me! It was Colin, you heard him. I didn't put the words in his mouth, did I?'

'No, but you sure gave him a mighty push.'

Ray heaved a sigh. His shoulders drooped helplessly. 'What was I supposed to do? Dad's onto this mayoralty thing, he wants it *bad.* 'I am taking the old fool down, he said. Get the rumours going!'

'I faked at first, told him that I'd done it. But he kept pressing. What did I say? Whom did I say it to? Why hasn't he heard people talking about it yet? Squeezing, sucking the air out of me, like a rope around my neck. No matter what I do, he'll get his way. He always does.'

'Yes, he does,' Arc repeated slowly. Arms around his bent knees, he set his gaze free, travelling over the grey-green colours of the hilltops. There was something magical in the landscape around here...an ingredient that made your thoughts run clear like a mountain stream. The big cities must be lacking it.

'But only because you *let him.*'

'Just think about it,' Arc urged. 'Before the bells, we were the ones to control the whole school, just the two of us. We said who deserved to live and who didn't. We caught the victims at the school gates, chewed them up and spat them out in a mushy slop. But how? How was it possible that only two of us were making the other 200 feel scared? It wasn't because we were stronger than the rest of them. It was because they DIDN'T BELIEVE THAT THEY WERE STRONG. Strong enough to say 'no' to us.'

Arc let his words sink in for a moment. His face remained solemn.

'The mayor's ideas are the right ones; we both know it, Ray. *He* was the one to get the town up and running after the winter disasters. And now *he*'s making sure that the power cut, the starving, and the rest of it won't happen again. There's also the new curriculum he's pushing through. The new subjects will mean a much better chance for us to do whatever we want to do with our lives. We'll be actually employable.'

Ray met Arc's intent stare. This time his words came out clear, slow, unwavering. 'So, no more…no more lies.' That was a promise.

A brilliant, impish smile flowered on Arc's lips. He gave his friend a satisfied slap on the shoulder and pulled his body up. With the air between them clear once again, it was time to see what the meeting was all about. Arc jerked his head in the direction of the Town Square:

'By the way, how many painting fingers have you got?'

'*Minus* ten,' Ray snickered and the boys tore down the hill, roaring with laughter.

That afternoon there were a couple of surprises waiting for them in the Town Square. The entire school seemed to have turned up; and so had most of the adults in the town. People were chatting excitedly, pointing at the façade where they imagined the two flying horses would be painted. A couple of metres away from the Town Hall's entrance there was a raised platform with a speaker stand. It was equipped with a microphone and covered in a blue cloth.

Arc and Ray made their way towards it, shuffling past familiar faces: Mrs Lavender, the queen of gossip, Mrs Phlox, the sweet shop owner, Mr Sage, the baker, some Year 8 and 7s. The boys' attention was soon drawn though by not who was here, but by who wasn't. The mayor. He was nowhere to be seen. Only his deputy and Mr Sedum were walking to and fro, sharing confused looks with each other near the raised platform. They were obviously waiting for the mayor to begin the whole thing. But where was he? Arc and Ray knew, from Jay, that he was the one driving the project forward.

With impatience dense into the air, Arc's dad finally left the speaker's platform and disappeared between the columns of the Town Hall. Soon he returned, the mayor walking by his side.15 minutes late.

John Sylvester scurried to the platform, cleared his throat and tapped the microphone with one finger to check if it was working.

'My dear fellows,' he said, 'you might not believe this but the clock in my office showed the wrong time! And that is just after I told off a member of staff for being late this morning because his cat chewed on his apple-strudel alarm. It must have smelled pretty darn well, that alarm. My apologies. Now back to what we are here to do…'

Arc was natural at reading faces. Ever since he was a little kid he could gauge accurately moods, tell what people were thinking. A crease over his father's left eyebrow would be a sign that he'd come home tired after a frustrating day at the Town Hall-that would be a bad time to ask him for toys. If his mum smiled and dimples appeared in the corners of her mouth, Arc could ask her safely to play outside till late. And at school…when the wimps' eyes got glued to the ground and their bodies shrivelled shamefully, Arc knew they were gone under for good.

He noticed now, standing taller than the throng around him, how people reacted to the mayor's joke. Some were amused, making little of the incident. But there also were others who shook their heads as though saying 'The old goof is losing it…'

The dismissal in the eyes of those people told Arc that the rumours, Ray's rumours, had already done a serious damage. This worried him a great deal. He didn't like the idea of somebody else taking Mr Sylvester's place, especially not Mr Sento. His old, acid self wouldn't be bothered. But the new Arc *knew*. He would miss the thrill of the new ideas coursing through his blood like liquid sunshine. He would miss that new town the mayor championed: that friendlier, self-sufficient, daring Stellaria, exploding with the colours of life. Ultimately, he would miss being his true self.

'Arc, Arc' Ray tugged at his friend's shoulder, 'where are you, man? They are asking for seniors to help with the grid measurements. Want to go?'

'Yeah.' It took Arc a few moments to resurface from his thoughts, 'Yeah, sure.'

The boys moved closer to the platform. Other people were doing the same and something on his left side caught Arc's eye. A boy and a girl were manoeuvring through the crowd, holding hands. The second surprise of the day! Mark, the boy Arc used to rag so roughly, and Dona, one of Nicole's circle. They stopped now: Mark was talking confidently, Dona hanging on his every word.

'Ray, take a look!' Arc indicated the unlikely couple with a twist of his head. 'Doesn't it seem strange to you? An ex-punch bag next to a bully's lapdog? '

'Lapcat, more like. We bit, they clawed. So, what, are they together now, like a boyfriend-girlfriend thing?'

'No, it can't be that,' Arc lowered his voice, as the couple moved closer to him and Ray. 'After the things he said to Nicole in maths, that's just not an option.'

Arc moved swiftly to intercept Mark and Dona.

'Hey, Mark,' came the light, buddy-like greeting, 'what's up?'

'Things are just grand. I've got my nice, green lily pad to chill on.'

Ah, the princess and the frog tease in maths! Arc and Ray guffawed, suddenly liking the guy standing in front of them: legs apart, hands easy by his hips, comically serious.

'Ray and I are volunteering for the Pegasus's grid. And you?' Arc asked.

'The same here,' Mark nodded. 'I was just explaining to Dona how the grid works. It has to do with ratios–'

'Perfect! Let's go together.' Arc winked secretly as a reply to the silent question in Ray's eyes. 'We just *have* to hear that explanation, don't we?'

Smug, Arc flung one arm around Ray's shoulders and the other one around Mark's. The boys made for the volunteers' queue. Dona was left out to trail behind them.

Chapter 14
The Best Laid Plans

She looked older than her age: hair pulled back into a neat chignon, eye-accentuating makeup and a black trouser suit to create the image of the perfect, loyal, city secretary. *Like mother, like daughter*, Sento thought. He wasn't fooled.

'What can I do for you, Miss Gentian?'

Nicole smoothed over the edge of her blazer and stood tall in front of the director's mahogany desk.

'I've come with a proposition, Mr Sento, one that will be advantageous to us both. We can help each other out, so to speak.'

'What makes you think I need any help?' Sento's black, predatory eyes flashed with a not-too-gentle warning. A director *ordered* something done, he didn't *ask* for it, nor did he ever make bargains–with girls.

'Well, your son for a start. He's not doing his job, is he? People are starting to think that the mayor is alright after all.'

'W-what?' Sento spluttered.

'I regret to be the one telling you this but...Ray hasn't been too subtle about spreading rumours around the school. I could trace every single one of them back to him, easily. But more to the point, he's not doing it anymore. And the buzz about the mayor doing things off his head is starting to die out.'

Though slightly trembling on the inside, Nicole met the director's hostile stare and held it. There was very little time before he considered her a threat and decided to deal with her accordingly. She had to convince him that they shared a common interest, and fast.

'Oration is everything I've ever known, Mr Sento. I've worked hard at it, ever since I was a little girl. Now when the Golden Muse is finally within my reach, the mayor's new curriculum is going to ruin everything. He'll have us soon playing football, and tennis, and wading in mud all over the Necklace Hills. Rumour has it that he's going to organise some new competition too, which will completely oust out the Golden Muse. Unless we elect a new mayor,' Nicole looked pointedly at Sento, 'oration will be wiped out of Stellaria, our traditions forgotten, our town turned into some insipid, common place. We can't let this happen, can we? If I take over from Ray I could tip the balance in your favour. Girls are naturally more skilled in the art of cunning subterfuge, as you will see.'

Wordless, the director regarded the girl in front of him for a few moments. He then gestured at her to take a seat in the armchair near the desk.

'Well, I see you've been keeping an eye on things, Nicole,' he said. 'A rather sharp eye.'

Nicole curled up her lip smugly. 'I've got some good ideas to go with that sharp eye, too. Sabotaging the Town Hall's mural, for example, will make a significant dent in the mayor's reputation. *'And Erie's'*, she thought. 'But what will take care of the problem, once and for all, will be going after the source. *The bellflowers.*'

The director's expression shifted. 'The flowers?'

'The moment they appeared in the Bells' house, things went haywire. The whole town changed! Not only the mayor, but my classmates too, my teachers, the baker, Mrs Phlox, even my own mother! Now they are all chasing after their ridiculous 'dreams,' Nicole scoffed. 'They even go and touch these flowers again and again, I am told, like a sort of pilgrimage, to have another dose of madness, no doubt.'

'I see. You and I are, then, the only sane people left.'

'The only ones I know of, yes.'

'And how do you suggest eliminating the bellflowers?'

Nicole leaned forward in the armchair, her expression foxy. 'Weedol. It's a pesticide easily found in the shed of, let's say, an amateur gardener. Gardening is one of the new hobbies people are taking up now. The pesticide contains an acid that destroys the plants' leaves. It fries them into crisps within a couple of hours.'

Mr Sento's fingers interlocked over his lap. His voice came back with a flicker of amusement.

'And you happen to know where such a shed can be found?'

'Oh, yes,' Nicole's voice fizzed with glee. Her mouth watered at the prospect of seeing Mark thrown to the mercy of these bellflower lovers. 'A rather annoying individual in my class needs to be taught a lesson. I hear he's been taking gardening lessons–from Erie, of course.'

Nicole left the factory, walking on clouds, jubilant. The director's words played in her head over and over again, like a catchy tune. 'If you prove as good as your word, or shall I say, if your *words* prove to be as good as you claim, well, we can come to an understanding. '

Chapter 15

Teaming up

Our eyes trained on the façade in front of us, we were willing the whole, gigantic thing to magically, by itself, fill in with colours and shapes.

'Big, huh,' Jay's breath blew out in a sharp gust. 'It sounded good when the mayor and Mrs Gentian were gushing about it …'

'But now it's waiting for *us*, Jay.' A jolt of unease pierced my stomach. 'Every single inch of it. '

A cone of sun rays suddenly spilled over the colonnaded entrance, blanketing the façade in golden haze. O*nly the sun can paint so elegantly in the blink of an eye,* I grunted in my head. Starting this Saturday morning we'd be lucky if our blue background would be done in a week.

'At least, we aren't alone anymore,' Jay said a little more cheerfully. 'Just look at this! She's gathered an army!'

I wheeled around towards the noises of chatter and shoes clumping over the cobblestones. Mrs Gentian had been knocking on quite a few sleepy doors, by the look of it, fetching the volunteers. Mr Penstemon and his son, Mr Sage, and hmm, Ray walking as usual by Arc's side, then Mark and Dona. 'I just hope he'll be as good with the brush as he is with fancy words,' I muttered, eyeing the oration king.

Mrs Gentian gathered us round. 'Well, guys, we are all here. Excited, aren't we? Imagine what it's going to look like when it's painted! Not only the white colour of the horses but also the blue, yellow and gold paints all around!'

'First things first though. We'll split into teams and, using chalk, draw a grid over the façade on both sides of the entrance. Here is how it works,' she showed us the drawing that Jay and I had prepared earlier.

'The mural on the left side of the entrance will look like this. You can see the grid over the picture, it has 2 by 2 inch squares. We are going to draw the same grid onto the facade, this time with 2.3 by 2.3 feet squares. Ms Marigold did all the calculations here, so they can't be anything but top-notch. The mural on the right side will be the exact mirror image. And for it we have another picture–this one.' Ms Gentian, or Tess, as she asked us to call her, let everybody have a look. For this painting Jay and I had used transparent paper. We'd traced the original Pegasus onto the paper, turned it over and traced the mirror image onto a new, white sheet of paper. 'Once we've done both grids, we can start transferring the painting square by square onto the wall.'

'Ehm, we are only doing the background, aren't we?' Ray inquired hesitantly. 'Because if I have to paint horses–'

'Oh, no, no way,' Tess chortled. 'We'll leave the horses to the masters.' She winked encouragingly at Jay and me. 'The girls will draw the shapes with chalk first, then they will paint them. The rest of us are here for the sky and the clouds only. Is everybody happy with that?'

Nods all around told her 'yes', so Tess and the mayor showed us how to use the step-ladders and paints safely. Soon after, we sat down to work out a schedule. Jay and I planned to work every day after school while the volunteers would come to help us on different days, whenever they could spare the time. Tess organised everything so well. By lunchtime all of us felt that when the mural was finished, it would be the best–the absolute best–thing we would have done in our lives!

Time glided into a starry night to flow into the next day like a river of smooth, velvety sunshine. The grid that the volunteers had laid was perfect. Jay and I used it to draw the first horse on the wall square by square, remembering ever so often to get down from the step-ladders and look at the picture from a distance. Ms Marigold had told Tess about it: it was the way to check that a mural of such a size didn't go wrong at some point. It was like people sometimes failing to see what's right in front of their noses.

By about 4 o'clock in the afternoon we finished, wondering if to call it a day when Dona and the boys showed up.

'Hey, why can't I hear any 'wow' and 'ah' noises yet?' Jay teased. 'Isn't it gorgeous?' She stepped back and gestured at the white wall behind us, crisscrossed with blue chalk lines. She did it so proudly as if the greatest ever masterpiece was already painted there.

'Wow, so huge and pretty!' Dona chirped.

Ray was more pragmatic. 'It's looking smashing, girls. Why don't we do some painting, now that we are here?'

'Well, why not?' Tess's glance travelled over our faces questioningly. 'If everybody's up for it, we can go to the storeroom. All the paint cans and brushes we need are there.'

Excited, we darted through the Town Hall's doors and up the stone staircase to the second floor. Tess joined us on the landing. 'That's the place,' she pointed to a door on the right. 'The mayor left the key with me.'

To our surprise, the wooden door to the storeroom was already ajar. It creaked open only with a slight push. Tess scowled before making her way in. 'This is not supposed to happen,' she muttered. The rest of the boys followed, then we, the girls.

The room filled in with our silent disbelief. All the cans of paint had been opened and left to dry. The colours inside were all mixed up: the blue with the yellow, the gold with white… The floor was covered with randomly thrown brushes, gloves and trays.

'I don't understand how someone can do something like that!' Dona exclaimed.

Stunned, Jay and I thought the same thing. Bur Arc snarled at her:

'Can't you? Isn't this the plan of your ringleader?'

'What…what are you talking about?' Dona mumbled. She took a step back, stumbling over a set of brushes.

'Now, wait, Arc! Dona's got nothing to do with this–' Mark protested.

'Hasn't she?' Arc, lurching, took a step closer to her. He stabbed an accusing finger in the air. 'Just ask her, why isn't she with the rest of Nicole's group? Why is she suddenly showing an interest in *you*? *Helping* us? '

The rest of us, standing up rigid, wide-eyed, waited for Dona to say something. We expected her to defend herself. But she didn't. She kept looking down, her eyes beginning to well up. Jay walked up to her and touched her on the arm, gently. 'Now, Dona, if you know something, anything, about what happened to the paint, you must tell us. The mural is too important to us. And to everyone else in town, Dona.'

'I-I-swear–I didn't do anything. I didn't even know where the paint was- until now.' Dona stifled down a sob and half-turned her face towards Mark:

'I'm sorry, I wanted to tell you. Nicole made me follow you, ' her voice faltered, '....to find out something embarrassing… so she can get back at you…But I don't want to do it. I don't. And I really want to help with the mural.'

Dona gave us one last, heartbroken glance before pelting out of the room.

Mark remained still, rooted to the spot, the hurt on his face beginning to mingle with some understanding. Ray gradually slouched, leaning his gangly body against a cupboard. Arc's eyes though were still narrowed, dripping suspicion:

'*She* might have not touched the paints, but I'm sure Nicole has.'

'And why are you so sure?' Tess was clearly offended, 'If you have something to say about my daughter, Arc, you'd better have some proof! '

Arc walked over to the door to close it shut. He came back.

'Mrs Gentian, Tess', he said uncomfortably, 'the last thing I want is to upset you... but Nicole... Well, let me explain. Mr Sento's been after the mayor these last months, hoodwinking people into believing Mr Sylvester's unfit for the position. Mr Sento wants the mayoralty–by hook or by crook. So, it's very likely he'll try to sabotage any of the mayor's projects that he can get his hands on...And the mural is one of them.' Arc gave us a pointed look. 'Ray and I had been keeping tabs on a few people though. We heard Nicole in school, talking to people. She was convincing them that their parents should vote for Mr Sento in the May election. Last week we even saw her going up to Senstar, to the director's office.'

'She went to Sento's office?' Tess's face fell. 'Why would she go there?'

'We don't know,' Ray answered this time. 'But we guess that it was either to report to him...or make some sort of a deal.'

Suddenly my mind went into overdrive. A collection of cogwheels started moving into space, whirring, fitting with each other. And then it all clicked.

'Um, guys, I've got to tell you something important,' I said. 'Remember in the autumn when Mr Lewelin kicked up that storm about the poisoned cocoa? That was for real.'

'What do you mean 'for real'? It was just a silly excuse to practise oration, wasn't it?' Ray grimaced.

'Nope. The lab tests proved that the level of pesticides was dangerously high. But if the factory were to close Mr Sento stood to lose too much–his money, his reputation, maybe even the whole business. So, he threw that oration bomb into town with the emergency committee. It all snowballed from there.' I met Arc's eyes. 'When we argued that day in school, I wasn't just trying to win an argument and look smart. I wanted to tell you the truth.'

'So why didn't you keep it up?' Ray drew in a deep breath. 'Why are you saying this now?'

'The town went mad so fast! Remember the winter food fights, the stabbings? Senstar got shut, so it wasn't making chocolates anyway. Then when the bellflowers appeared, I was too optimistic. I hoped people, and most of all, Mr Sento, would only want to do the right thing…'

Jay took over from me, her voice brimming now with determination.

'But it's getting worse now, much worse. Mr Sento has not only been keeping quiet about the chocolates, he's been spreading his net further, onto the mayor and our mural. We can't just sit back and do nothing! We've got to stop him!'

'*We* can't do much on our own, but if the whole town stood up to him–' Arc piped up.

'No, wait! You have no real proof. Yet,' Tess warned. 'It all makes sense, I agree, and it's very likely that Sento is planning to get the most influential position in town: the mayoralty. Erie, has your mum still got the scientist's reports?'

'No, that's the thing,' my words came out gloomy. 'Mr Sento asked her to return the reports to him; nobody's seen them since.'

'Then I'll speak to the mayor. We *are going* to deal with it, you have my word.' The resolve in Tess's eyes mingled with an aching regret. 'I'm sorry, Ray, but we *have to.* He's your father, I know how that feels..... Nicole is my family too. But she'll *have to tell* me everything she knows.'

Chapter 16
Rising up

Philius Sento opened the door of the office to notice a new envelope on his desk. The red-and-white logo on top was bad news. *Damn it!* The control over the factory felt like a slimy fish slipping away from his hands.

'Thomson!' he bellowed out.

The manager's burly torso couldn't move very fast. Even so, he appeared in front of the green velvet desk in less than a minute. His black hair, slicked over his elongated forehead, fitted with the rest of him resembling an overfed Doberman.

'If anybody asks, I haven't received any letters from the HSE. We are continuing as usual, using our existing stock of cocoa powder. Which is perfectly safe!' Sento shot a warning look. 'Understood?'

'Yes, Mr Sento,' came Thomson's grovel.

'Somebody might come in person, if they can be bothered. In that case, spread the rumour that concerned workers have been protecting the factory. They have been destroying all letters containing *unjust* warnings and *unproven* accusations of poisoning. I know nothing about it. And neither do you.'

Thomson nodded gravely.

'Now, I've got some business to take care of. I don't want anybody disturbing me. '

Philius Sento gave instructions to the manager to oversee the production for the morning. He then shut himself in his expensive office, wearing his expensive suit and got thinking.

While the chocolate factory was significant in the gradual recovery of the town, the mayor planned to reduce its future influence by diversifying. Being almost entirely dependent on a single business made Stellaria vulnerable. This winter's cease of production had proven that: Sento had come very close to losing all his contracts. It would be better if the town had other ventures and became more self-sufficient. Growing a few fruits and vegetables, perhaps, now that the spring was so warm. A free-range chicken farm; a business that could thrive in winter. Why not build a ski resort?

The letter that lay open on John Sylvester's desk on that mid-March afternoon was one more proof why he needed to take action. The HSE was giving Senstar a final notice to stop using the pesticide-contaminated cocoa. In case of non-compliance, a financial penalty would be reinforced, it said, and that would increase with each day.

The news was deeply troubling. The mayor re-read the letter for the third time, the crease in the middle of his forehead taut with emotions and thoughts. So, it turned out that Sento had been playing a dangerous game behind his back. He had been keeping the threat of poisoning hush-hush. Nobody, nobody in Stellaria had any idea of that. The cocoa contamination, by what the HSE was saying, was now as real as the logo-printed paper John Sylvester was clutching in his hands.

Finally, the mayor made up his mind. He strode purposely out of the Town Hall, heading straight for Senstar and Sento's office. When he opened the first door, the emptiness of the secretary's office surprised him.

'Is this his way to avoid visitors?' the mayor wondered. He walked across the room before his hand closed around the second door's handle, pressing down. The door was locked.

'The director receives visitors by appointment only. If you come through to my office, I will book one for you at the earliest convenience, Mr Sylvester.'

The mayor turned around. His eyes flashed warningly, staring at the factory's manager.

'I'm here on an *urgent* matter, Mr Thomson. There can't be any delays.'

'I am afraid I cannot help you. Mr Sento is out on important business.'

'Is he? What could be more important than this?' the mayor waved the letter in his hand dangerously close to Thomson's eyes. His voice rose-demanding, threatening. 'Is this business about *saving the factory* or not?'

Thomson's guard-dog features sharpened. He took another step towards the mayor. ''Senstar is in perfectly good hands, mayor. I assure you. And I don't–'

John Sylvester slammed his fist into the director's door. His yells weren't uncontrolled spite like they'd been during the winter siege. Now they were full of cold, thought-out determination. 'If you are here, open that door, Sento! Or *I* will let all the workers know about the HSE's letter!'

The *click-click* noise of a key turning into the keyhole preceded Sento's grim voice by a few seconds. 'Very well... Come inside.'

'The same bomb has been dropped on your desk, I see,' the mayor began, glancing at a letter identical to the one in his hand. He took a seat without waiting to be invited. 'What I want to know is why haven't you done anything these months? And what do you intend to do now?'

Sento walked around the desk and sat down opposite the mayor. His confidence was somehow shaken but his mind was already calculating the next move.

'I thought we all agreed that the poisoning was fictitious, John. Not a single piece of credible evidence. All the debates here and in the town square… You played a rather major part in refuting the claims of that scientist, as I recall.'

'This was before. And *this*,' the mayor stabbed the letter lying on the desk with his finger, 'is NOW! Why didn't you tell us about the new evidence? The town has the right to know if we're churning out poisonous chocolates, don't you think?'

'It's an exaggeration, a money-making machine for the government.'

'Sento, you are PUTTING PEOPLE'S HEALTH AT RISK! That's no exaggeration! I want your assurance that you'll arrange for a new batch of cocoa powder to be purchased. AND YOU'LL DO THAT TODAY!'

'I'll do everything that is in Senstar's best interests,' Sento said evasively.

'And what does this mean exactly? That you're going to keep using the cheap cocoa? The one laden with pesticides?'

The director didn't reply.

'May I remind you of my position, Sento! I could rally the whole town behind me and leave you no option but to do what is right!'

'And may I remind you that the mayor's elections are drawing closer! You have outlived your usefulness to the town!'

The mayor rose from his seat. Slowly, he leaned over the desk and its short, now slightly cowering, owner.

'If you want to play that game, *we will,* Sento. We'll play it long enough for you to lose every last shred of credibility in this town.'

He stormed out of the room without so much as another word. His face was like a lightning before a thunder, as he walked through the production rooms. People noticed him, called out to him but in vain. The mayor ignored them, needing a place to calm down and consider his next move. Needing the inspiration of the bellflowers.

In the mixing room he was joined by Angelina Bell.

'My shift's just ended, mayor,' she said quietly, falling into step beside him. 'I'll walk with you, if you don't mind'.

John Sylvester just gave a slight nod.

They left Senstar and followed the path between the spruce trees for nearly a quarter of an hour. In the troubled silence hanging between them, the mayor fought to regain control over his thoughts and emotions. Angelina, on the other hand, contemplated the far-from-good news she had to deliver to him. She could feel how it would add to the pressure he was already under. If she was that distraught, the first thing she would do was…The mayor's destination became apparent to her even before the swan cottage itself came into view. Ribbons of bellflowers crisscrossed in all directions, vividly blue against the white walls.

'It is amazing how these bells never diminish. They are being replaced by new ones, aren't they? Every time a flower is damaged or wilts, a new one grows in its place.' John Sylvester turned to look at Angelina and saw the confirmation of his words on her face. Then he ran his hand over the blossoms, wondering if their powers would be as strong and instantaneous as they'd been that first day.

Yes, they were. Even more so. His mind cleared up before he had time to remember the moans of the wounded house, and the past vengeance of menacing shovels and axes. The flowers were guarding the Bells' cottage now, guarding all of Stellaria, against another such surge of annihilating madness.

Angelina Bell had seen many of her fellow Stellarians coming to the house in the last months, repeating the same gesture. Recharging, firing their imagination, and shaking negativity off like an old, wrinkled skin. The flowers put a smile on her own face, too, from the moment she woke up in the morning till the moment she closed eyes in a peaceful sleep. Angelina just hoped that this would never change.

'There's something you should know, John,' she said, judging that now it was as good a time as any to break her news. 'On the quiet, one by one, the manager has been threatening the workers in Senstar. He is saying that if we don't vote for Sento being the new mayor, we'll lose our jobs.'

'After the meeting I've had with him,' the mayor fixed his serious blue eyes on hers, 'this comes as no surprise. Sento even had a go at me–as if I had anything to lose. I'd gladly clear the way for someone talented, and– the mayor chuckled self-deprecatingly 'and hopefully younger than me. But definitely not Sento! He's venomous! He's going to *ruin* our town.'

'He's planning something horrible, isn't he?' guessed Angelina. Her face tensed with anxiety.

'Yes,' the mayor nodded solemnly, 'he's determined to keep the production at a low cost, even if that means poisoning people in the process.

And I'm going,' he interrupted Angelina's rising up question; 'to let everybody know about this at a meeting in the Town Hall. Thank you, Angelina, for everything.'

Chapter 17
Cloak-and –dagger

The following week glided in on the light, comfortable note of normality. It was all part of a strategically planned warfare against the Senstar's conniving director.

At six o'clock the morning shift workers filed into the mixing, moulding and packing rooms, chatting animatedly and starting the production as routinely as they did every day. Mr Sento did the customary cold-stare, inspection rounds and retired to his office. Not anticipating any visitors or troubles, he left the key to the office untouched inside its keyhole.

The director's cup of steaming coffee was hardly diminished by half when the first disaster struck.

'Good morning, Mr Sento,' the quality controller said. He *had* knocked on the office door before letting himself in.

'Ah, Bellis …what a surprise!' Sento managed to half-mumble.

You've got no idea what a surprise this really is!

'You should report to Mr Thomson, Bellis, on all matters regarding the quality of the chocolates.'

'The chocolates are per-rr-fection, Mr Sento. It's the small matter of my resignation that I'm here for,' Tom said with levity. He was a middle-aged man who had always worn a serious, rather strict expression. But now the new, mischievous smile made him look much younger than his age. 'You see, orchards have been a hobby of mine for quite some time now. So, I've decided to turn the hobby into a full-time occupation. You are looking at the manager of Mrs Lavender's new cherry and apple orchard!'

'What? What's all this nonsense? What are you blabbering about?' Mr Sento hollered.

'I'm moving on, Mr Sento. I feel it's time for a change,' Tom's eyes flickered, suggesting that it wasn't him in need of a real change but that other person behind the office desk. He placed a gleaming white envelope on the director's desk. 'Well, that's all, I believe. This is my resignation. It's been, hmm, enlightening, working for you, Mr Sento and now I must bid you good day.' With that Tom let himself out of the office, ignoring the livid yells behind him:

'Bellis, come back! Right this minute! Your contract binds you to giving a month's notice!'

'Mr Sento?' The manager now entered the office, having walked down the corridor from the packing room. He was on his way to inspect an order for the City when he heard the director's screams. 'What's Bellis been saying? If he's forgotten where his place is, I'd be happy to refresh his memory.' Rob Thomson made sure the door was tightly shut and the office insulated against prying ears before he offered his services.

'No, no need for that,' rather flushed, Sento ran a hand through his receding grey hair. 'I suppose, I can put Chris Thymus in his place. The other workers in the mixing room can make up for the absence of one man somehow; perhaps work a slightly longer shift…'

While Mr Sento was considering the idea and wondering just how all this had come about, Chris Thymus himself– a tall, lean, dark-haired man in his thirties–appeared at the office door.

Splendid! The good old fellow is coming to the office even before being called! Things are finally returning to normal. Everything and everybody here is under my control! The director smiled a practised, suave smile.

'Ah, Thymus, just the man I need! Now, there is an excellent, excellent opportunity for you to be promoted. The post of quality controller comes with more responsibilities, and,' Mr Sento stared meaningfully at his employee, 'with a significant pay rise.'

'Thank you for the offer, Mr Sento, but I must decline. I actually came to resign from my job.'

'NO! NO! You wouldn't dare! What is this? Some kind of plot to ruin Senstar?' screeched the director. He shot up from his seat so fast that the entire office quaked. This was all too much to be a coincidence.

'My granddad left me some money. I'm thinking of opening a shoemaking shop,' came Thymus's nonchalant, overly polite response. In fact, he was secretly gloating. 'My grandpa was a talented cobbler. He taught me when I was a young lad. It will be grand to revive his craft now. So, um, good day to you.'

Chris Thymus left, whistling a merry tune, unruffled by the director's and the manager's protests.

His actions were repeated by the entire morning-shift staff who declared newly found passions for glass–making, carpet weaving and all other sorts of jobs, 'bizarre' for their suddenness.

Mr Sento's last glimmer of hope that things would be different in the midday shift was extinguished with the appearance of Angelina Bell.

She announced her taking on the new role of patisserie chef. Then, as though that wasn't enough, Samuel Penstemon arrived with the news that he was joining the family business and was going to give a hand to his dad with a large order of wooden chairs for the Town Hall.

The workers just kept leaving…At the end of the day the factory's director and manager found themselves all alone in the mixing room, staring blankly into the abandoned containers of solidified chocolate. The bonbon trays and glitzy boxes in the room beyond were equally vacant.

For the first time in his life Philius Sento felt like a failure. The thought festered in him, gnawed deeper, and poisoned him to his very blood and bones. He couldn't fight it. Only deny it.

'This is not happening. Not happening! It's all a nightmare! I'll wake up from it any minute,' he mumbled. Next to him, Rob Thomson didn't appear to be able to hear anything. He had the resigned stillness of a person trapped into quicksand, expecting the final pull down…

After a sleepless night, spent in the red velvet armchair in front of his lavishly decorated fireplace at home, Mr Sento mustered the courage to return to Senstar the next day. He had managed to regain some of his self-complacency. '*They are bluffing, they must be bluffing,*' he had convinced himself. They couldn't have possibly made plans for all these new ventures overnight. Starting a new business was no child's play; being a businessman himself, he knew very well the kind of preparations it took. Yes, Mr Sento thought more and more confidently, climbing up the spruce-clad slope towards Senstar, this was all a ploy depending on his quick surrender. But he *wasn't* going to surrender. He was going to bid his time patiently, and after a few days they would come begging him for their old jobs. *Begging him!*

Senstar was silent and devoid of human presence. Grim, dark-bricked, it stood up like an ancient citadel that time had made irrelevant and useless. For half a century it had been the heart of Stellaria's trade but now it lay deserted, betrayed by the very same people that once had cherished it. This could not be the end; it could not…

Sento waited in his office, his bastion of power, for hours on end. He expected a knock on the door that would herald his victory and the humiliating defeat of his insubordinate workers. Mr Thomson joined him as the sun climbed up to its zenith.

'How are you bearing up, Mr Sento?' the manager inquired, taking a seat by the desk. 'I don't think they'll be able to keep it up for much longer.'

'Yes, yes,' the director said irritably, 'but where are they? What are they doing? Why aren't they coming back?'

'I have been checking up on that actually. I saw Luke Diascia, the new boy from the moulding room, helping in the bakery. Does he think baking bread pays better than making our chocolates? He's got a lot to learn...And Star Primrose, the pretty girl, working in the packing room, is now messing with some paint at the Town Hall...'

'It's just a bluff. It can't be anything else. If they think that they'll get the better of me...'

Philius Sento spitted the words through gritted teeth. Then, not being able to bear the suspense anymore, he stood up abruptly and commanded, 'You stay here, Thomson, in case they start coming back. I'll go out there and see, with my own eyes, just what these people are playing at.'

His investigative tour of the town confirmed Mr Thomson's news. Everybody who should be normally working in Senstar wasn't. Wherever he went, Mr Sento saw the happy faces of people in the buzz of activity, perfectly content with some new arrangements. The workers, *his* workers, seemed to have forgotten the very existence of the chocolate factory! And its director, for this matter! Here and there he received a nod of the head in acknowledgement and a distant 'Good Afternoon!' but otherwise there weren't any frantic souls, sobbing and pleading with him to rescue them from the hardships of impecuniousness.

He had to leave. He had to leave it all behind because he couldn't stand the normality of it all: the seven Necklace Hills serenely rising up towards the limpid-blue skies; the thrills of mistle thrushes filling up the air; the people, the streets, the buildings…Life flowed as effortlessly as ever-without *him*.

His strained, harried retreat didn't go unobserved though. Two people standing at the arched entrance to the Town Hall watched him walk across the square and climb up a cobble street to the left until he disappeared from view behind the trees. The future, and what it held for all of them, weighed on their minds.

'Do you reckon he'll hold on for much longer?' the deputy mayor asked.

'My guess is a few more days. His city clients are going to raise a rumpus any day now,' the mayor replied. 'Sento will have to restart production if Senstar's going to survive.'

'He suspects the bluff then?'

'Yes, I think, but he is not absolutely sure of it. That's what we count on. Let's hope the factory staff will continue giving brilliant performances until his patience or,' the mayor smiled humourlessly, 'his stubbornness runs out.'

'But they actually plan on returning to Senstar, don't they? Even though it all began as a hoax, it looks rather convincing now. This morning when I went to the bakery, Sage's apprentice was making sesame bagels. The lad's got a real flair for it. And his bagels are the best I've ever tasted!'

John Sylvester was pleased, 'A lot of people might find their hidden talents before all of this is over. But a lot will also continue making chocolates. Stellaria won't be the same without the chocolate factory. I must admit, though,' a scowl clouded the mayor's face, 'that I'd love to see a new director running it. Or at least a new Sento.'

'And so would I,' Eric Libertia agreed. 'I really can't get my head around the way he's been these three months. As far as I can tell, the bellflowers drained the madness out of all of us. But not him. It's as though the flowers didn't affect him at all.'

'I think… that they did.'

The mayor stared ahead into the distance, thinking, his eyes trailing the waves of hills.

'But he wasn't ready for it, for letting go of the way he'd been thinking all his life. He grew up, you see, with the idea of being the son of the most important person in town. And then he himself became that person. So, his ego… has always been of the carnivorous kind. '

John turned to look at his deputy, his expression sombre.

'When you are so preoccupied with yourself,' he went on, 'you can hardly notice the others around you. Notice them longer, that is, than the time it takes you to intimidate them, knock them down or crush them beneath your feet. Life gets to be a bloody, flesh-ripping competition. But what *if it isn't,* Eric? What if it doesn't have to be? Mrs Gentian has been telling me about nature these past months, about how different species *live together.* That's called symbiosis. You'll find TV documentaries often talking about predation and competition between species. But now scientists are also recognising the importance of cooperation, too.'

Eric seemed to remember something.

'Wait,' he said, 'this rings a bell. I saw a clip of this movie, *Fantastic Fungi.* Apparently, 80% of plants are in symbiosis with fungi. The fungi help with the absorption of water and minerals. In turn, the plants supply them with carbohydrates. It's a win-win!'

'Precisely. Coral reefs, too, are symbiosis in action…'

The mayor went silent with surfacing realisation. His features sharpened and his eyes now burned with new intensity.

'People like Sento will tell you that it's dog eating dog out there…But the truth might be rather something else, Eric. The truth might be that life is full of possibilities not because of dog fights but because of species working together. Because of *people* working together.'

Eric Libertia's eyes shone with excitement at these words.

'John, that's exactly how I felt at the Bells' when the flowers burst out! Take our swan town, for example. It started out with a dream, didn't it? Alex Bell's dream. Our parents got together and built the swan cottages. The dream came true and everybody enjoyed it. It's a legacy we'll leave to our children.'

'Come to think of it,' John added, 'it's the same with any other place on earth. In an American city, white and black people dining in the same restaurant-that's the legacy of the civil movement led by Martin Luther King; an election day in London and women voting next to men-the legacy of the suffragette movement; fascinating skyscrapers, sleek speedy trains, serene temples, scenic parks…None of these could have been possible by the effort of a single person.'

Life is short, people say. True. But even in the shortest of life spans you'll always have time to do two things: first, *have a brilliant idea* and second, be *part of a team that makes a brilliant idea come true*.

Epilogue

The trills of the mistle thrushes burst, fade, and then burst again in the breeze. On a day like this, boundaries seem to melt at the edges, links appear tangible. The boulder underneath me takes on the hue of the swishing grass … Green spruces and golden rays weave into the sky brocade and swan houses seep their whiteness into the hills. My town is a part of everything else and everything else is a part of my town...

I am perched, like a bird at the top of the third Necklace Hill. There is no better place to feel the heartbeat of my new Stellaria, to see how much it has changed. The Town Square is alive with people drawn to the new patisserie by the aroma of sweet baking. The building is crafted out of honey-coloured pine wood: in the shape of an octagon, with a conical roof. The interior, designed beautifully in the colours of the sea, is Mrs Phlox's. Ships at sea, I remember her saying, ships that plough the rolling waves are symbols of our lives' journeys.

So many dreams have been born in my town since my last birthday, since the bellflowers: it takes my breath away. Down below, on the front of the Town Hall, blossoms, like a flower, my best friend's dream. The mural had brought all of us closer together. When the paint turned up ruined, it was Arc who first began unravelling the threads of Sento's and Nicole's conspiracies. The entire machinations were soon exposed at that unforgettable, rebellious town meeting that ended with such a brilliant plan! Our cloak-and-dagger game made Sento capitulate in a week. At the same time, Tess stopped the idea of the Weedol murder in its tracks, making sure all sheds were safely locked away.

So, by the time the Spring Party lit the Town Square with colourful paper lanterns and live music, we had not one but two victories to celebrate. The first was the splendour of the two Pegasuses. The second–the election of the Stellarian Citizen Committee (SCC) which is chaired, of course, by Mum. She's no stranger to chairing committees, after all. The SCC was set to monitor the running of Senstar and step in when concerns were raised by the workers, or generally by any Stellarians.

Its first ultimatum, no kid's gloves here, was for Sento to replace the contaminated cocoa with a new, pesticide-free batch. The committee went all the way to London with him to make sure that he did just that! Now, gazing at the tall chimneys of Senstar, my breathing is unbelievably light and effortless. My thoughts are light, too, not weighed down by a poison.

I hear voices cartwheeling over each other in the air, ringing my name. I swing towards the birch trees on my right and smile. I don't even need to see them, their voices are so familiar, so heart-warming. Three colourful dots emerge on the black-and-white canvas of tree trunks. Lemon-saffron streaks shimmer through it, courtesy of the early August sun.

'Hey, there, stranger,' Jay twits, waving a hand. There's a spring in her step, thanks to all these school trips to the Necklace Hills that Tess's new curriculum made possible. Even the boys, with their crane-like legs, have a hard time catching up with her.

'Your mum sent us looking for you; she needs help in the patisserie.'

'So, we thought,' Arc is panting slightly, now that he's climbed to the top of the hill, 'that you must be here, ogling the mountains.'

An impish smile tugs at the corners of Ray's mouth. 'Hatching a new, crazy plot to plant flowers somewhere, no doubt.'

Arc shoots him a pointed look and Ray's expression gets sheepish. The boys lead the way down the hill and onto the Town Square, as Jay and I babble on. People are flocking to the patisserie in their dozens and I think that Mum will be glad of some extra help. Perhaps, we could all–

Wait! The din is on the opposite side of the square. There's a stage set up there and a banner spans over it, decorated with silk flowers. The banner has enormous silver letters reading 'Stellaria Annual Flower Garden Competition'.

A thought flickers at the back of my mind, gets stronger and brighter. So, all of these new gardens around town, people asking me how to start planting hyacinths, roses, lavender and cornflowers…

'You've been chosen to cut the ribbon on stage and unveil the competition, Erie!' Jay trills. Her arms take me in the hugest of hugs.

'And you're also the head judge,' Ray joins in.

Arc can't resist a wisecrack, 'So, brace yourself for flower-mad people chasing you around town for years and years on end.'

The flower mad-people are shaking both my hands now, swaying and ebbing around me like the waves of the ocean. Their eyes are shining with joy. Mum and Dad are making their way through the crowd. Mr Sylvester's placing a magenta sash around my shoulders, ushering me towards the stage…

I feel sails unfurling in my heart, an anchor rising from depths of the waves. My journey is about to begin. And I'm now well prepared to be the captain of my ship. *Of my life.*

Acknowledgements:

I would like to thank from the bottom of my heart Lyn and Afaf, my beta-readers, for their warm encouragement and valuable advice. Erie's story is now a better one because of them.

About the author:

Violeta loves mountains, flowers and trees, especially these in her home country, Bulgaria. Her interests lie in school education as well as new technologies related to environmental protection.

Coming up soon:

Interconnected: A collection of short stories (e-book)

Blog: violetsanswers.blogspot.com/